SHADOW MOUNTAIN

SHADOW MOUNTAIN

B. M. Bower

GUNSMOKE

First published in the UK by Collins

This hardback edition 2012
by AudioGO Ltd
by arrangement with
Golden West Literary Agency

ISBN 978 1 445 82416 1

British Library Cataloguing in Publication Data available.

Printed and bound in Great Britain by
MPG Books Group Limited

THE MOUNTAIN

SEEN IN FULL DAYLIGHT, especially from the eastern side, the high peak called Shadow Mountain was not remarkable. In that land of erosions and strange volcanic formations, hills often bore strange likenesses to castles, grotesque animals, anything a man's imagination might make of them. In daylight, Shadow Mountain showed a knobby peak on its northern crest, sloping sharply down to a saddle where the wind whistled. Then, south of the depression, a sharp pinnacle jutted out and up like a stubby horn. If the outline resembled anything at all it was a setting hen with the mumps, and even that would be a long stretch of the imagination.

Just before the sun dropped out of sight behind the low hills to the west, however, Shadow Mountain revealed the reason for its name. Then it painted the perfect shadow of a human form upon the wide deep valley to the east: the gigantic figure of a monk, hooded and with his draped right arm lifted to point toward Cherry Creek flowing placidly across the eastern end of the basin. With the changing seasons which sent the sunsets creeping north and back again, that shadow finger moved imperceptibly across the valley's mouth. Seen from the high bench on either side, the likeness was rather startling, and to an imaginative mind sinister.

According to the old-timers, no Indian would enter the valley called Shadow Mountain Basin after the sun had left the midheavens. They had a legend that told how and why that shadow fell upon the valley. It proved beyond all argument that the finger always pointed to

1

trouble. If it fell upon a man, that was very bad medicine. He would have sickness, perhaps even death ; in any case he might be sure that black days would be his fate for many moons afterwards. It was wise to ride around that valley and not to tempt that Black One to work his evil spell.

True or false, the superstition did not die altogether when the Indians left that territory, making way for the white man's herds. There were white men, especially among the older ones, who half believed it even though they would strenuously deny the charge.

When the Triangle J moved in and took possession of the basin for a winter range, they did so from the age-old impulse to take and hold that which seems good. Not often does a man find a spot made perfect by Nature for his purpose (as if she had worked under his orders) ; when he does, he feels that it is his by divine right, and he possesses it if he can.

So John Coleson, riding to the edge of the bench and looking down into the valley at the close of a day's scouting over his new cattle range, saw the Basin lying there empty, just waiting for his acceptance: a place such as he had always dreamed about but never before had seen except in some other man's grasp.

Easing himself in the saddle, he glanced at the cowboy who had pulled up beside him. "The Lord sure made that basin down there for cattle, Jerry," he declared with an undertone of excitement. "There's my winter range, sure as you're born."

"You're darn whistlin'," Jerry agreed, licking down the cigarette he had just rolled. His eyes took in the full expanse of high-walled valley, watered by no less than three small creeks fed by springs from Shadow Mountain. "Winter range till kingdom-come, John. You

2

can winter every hoof you own in here and never lose a critter, unless it's by accident."

"That's right," assented his boss. "I'll build me a line camp down there at the mouth of the valley on the river, and two men can handle the whole thing. It's a cinch."

At once they began to estimate the number of cattle the Basin would support through the winter, and just where the line camp should be built. And although the Black One was pointing straight at the spot Coleson finally chose, neither noticed the shadow's human likeness, nor would have cared anything about it if he had.

Yet Coleson noticed how black it lay, and long. "Getting close to sundown, Jerry," he observed, taking up the slack in his bridle reins. "We better be driftin'. We'll be in the dark getting home."

That is how the Triangle J took possession of Shadow Mountain Basin. In that wide-open land there was none to dispute the taking by right of discovery. As yet the Basin was unknown to surveyors, unmarked by cornerstone or section number: virgin land, where antelope grazed in herds and where wolves had their dens in the rocky walls that were too steep and high for cattle to climb, except where Cherry Creek flowed past in its own brushy bottomland, and the bench sloped down easily to the flat bottom. It was to hold the stock back from drifting up or down the creek that the line camp was needed.

There in the Basin the grass grew thick and high and ripened sweetly in the fall, and the winter snows drifted only against the south wall. The cattle fattened through the cold weather, full-fed, protected from the bitter winds that raged across the benches, and the calves they dropped were strong. The Triangle J came to be

3

reckoned a big outfit even in that land where cattle were counted by thousands, and Coleson's riders bore themselves jauntily, content with life as they found it here.

Day after day when the sky was free of clouds, the black-cowled shadow laid its fingertip upon the Triangle J line camp, and no harm came of it. To the cowboys it was just a reminder that day was done. If it meant anything at all it meant suppertime; certainly nothing more portentous.

THE BLACK ONE POINTS

But THERE WAS ONE PERSON at the Triangle J, the girl who had grown up there, who sometimes played with the superstition of the Black One's shadow, just to bedevil any poor cowboy who would argue the point. Certainly she could not have taken the old Indian legend seriously, especially now when she was twenty-two and had just finished a sophisticating four years at the State University. Not even being named Demeter in honor of a goddess by her bookishly inclined mother could have made her believe in the legend. But she never missed a chance of watching it, for all that.

So it was not simply to hector the strikingly handsome young man beside her that she reined abruptly out of the trail they were following and sent her horse galloping straight out across the bench to the edge where it sloped down to Cherry Creek.

Big Paul Ganzer spilled all the tobacco out of the cigarette he was rolling when his horse leaped to follow.

"Hey! Where yuh going, Demmy?" he shouted, leaning to the chase. "I thought you was in a grand rush

4

to get home!"

Demmy lifted an arm and pointed. "The sun, Pollo! It's going to set!"

"Hunh! Think you can stop it from settin'? They learn yuh that trick in college?"

As he surged up alongside, Demmy turned her head and scrutinized him with narrowed eyes. "Sometimes, Pollo, I wonder whether you really are dumb, or whether you're just being smart. You're Apollo to look at, but sometimes I suspect you're just Caliban inside. Are you?" Her eyes mocked him.

The big fellow shook his head, looking secretly flattered. "Well, if Caliban's the kinda feller that felt a lot more than he ever let on, you can take it from me I'm him, all right. Deep down inside me, Demmy, I— Well, ever since you come home this last time, I—"

Demmy's laugh was like a yanked rein, stopping him on the brink of confession.

"Oh, don't go floundering up to your eyebrows in sentiment—you spoil the picture."

"Aw, you always kid a fellow till he don't know whether he's going or coming. Honest, Demmy—"

"Hold your head up, a bit sidewise, Pollo. Riding with the sun on your face like that, you're absolutely the most godlike-looking creature I ever saw in my life. You—well, you look positively gilded, like a temple dome—or a tin roof."

Pollo broke the pose he had obediently taken, and the flush that darkened his face was not the work of the sun. He jerked the reins, riding in closer to the girl.

"Say, you never turn loose a compliment lately without tying a tin can to its tail. That damned college has just about ruined the sweetest girl that ever lived! Ever since you come home, there's a slam in everything

5

you say. By gosh, if you think you can high-hat me and get away with it, just because I'm only a plain cowpuncher—"

"Not plain, Pollo! By no stretch of the imagination plain!"

"There you go again! Don't yuh know you can't fool with me always the way you're doing?" Abruptly he reached out and caught her around her slim belted waist, half lifting her from the saddle. "If you like me, Demmy—for God sake quit tormentin' me!"

With the swift strong suppleness of a wild thing caught unawares, the girl writhed somehow away from his embrace. Gripping the saddle horn she righted herself. Her eyes were furious, with a startled look behind her anger. But her voice showed only a sharp distaste.

"Mind your manners, Paul Ganzer. Where's your sense of humor, for heavens' sake? If you're going to get all excited over a little wisecracking, I'll have to find an escort who can take a joke." She watched him from the corner of her eye, and kept her horse at a lope with plenty of space between them.

Paul Ganzer had his handsome black eyebrows pulled together. "I can take a joke as well as the next one. But folks don't do much wisecrackin' about my looks," he retorted sullenly. "It ain't my fault if I'm—" He stuck there, groping for a word.

"No, it isn't your fault if you're simply too handsome to live, I suppose," Demmy finished for him sarcastically. "Well, handsome is as handsome does. Don't be a complete sap, is all I ask." She faced forward, dismissing the subject with a gesture. "Come on. I want to see the Black One again."

"Hunh? Whatcha mean, Black One?"

6

Demmy did not answer. She was off at a sharp gallop again, riding with the unthinking limber grace of a boy on some exciting quest; galloping recklessly among the scattered rocks half buried in the sod along the Basin's rim, trusting to the sure-footedness of her horse. As she rode the anger left her eyes. She was laughing in good humor again when they pulled up at the brow of the hill.

"There he is, Pollo, large as life. The Black One pointing his finger of doom—"

"Say! You mean that shadow? Hunh! If that was the finger of doom, I'd 'a' been dead long ago. There ain't a word of truth in that old yarn, Demmy, and you know it as well as I do."

"You don't know anything about it. You've only been working for Dad a couple of years or so, and the Black One never hurries his dooming." The glint in her eyes should have warned him she was baiting him again. "You know what Omar says about it:—

The Moving Finger writes; and having writ,
Moves on; nor all your Piety nor Wit
   Shall lure it back to cancel half a Line,
Nor all your Tears wash out a Word of it.

You'd think old Omar had the Black One in mind, wouldn't you? Because that's exactly what that shadow is like."

"Well, I don't know the jasper, but he sure better not go shooting off his face like that around me," snorted Pollo, with a dull man's resentment for anything he cannot understand. "That's all hooey."

"I wouldn't be too sure of that, if I were you." But Demmy was biting back an impish grin. "Oh, look! Who's that coming down the creek? He's riding smack

7

under the Black One's finger. Why don't you yell at him, Pollo? Tell him to wait till the sun's gone down before he goes any farther. If he's a stranger and doesn't know about the curse, we shouldn't let him ride right into it without warning him, should we?"

"The heck we shouldn't! There ain't anything in it, and if there was, he can take his chance same as anybody. I've rode into that shadow more times than I can count, and I ain't dead yet."

"But you will be. You just wait!"

"Quit your kiddin'. I'll wait a long time, then. Even if it did bring a curse, that's his funeral; not mine."

Demmy turned her head and looked at him as if he had suddenly become a total stranger to her. "I believe," she said slowly, "you actually mean that, Pollo."

Pollo looked blank. "Sure, I mean it. Fellow I never saw before—I'd look swell, wouldn't I, worryin' over him headin' into trouble maybe? You've got some funny notions, Demmy. I never saw a girl like you."

"I think you're the one with funny notions. Did you ever in your life do anything for someone else—anything that wouldn't benefit you, at least indirectly?" She was studying him curiously. Her voice had nothing in it now of bantering.

"I'd do anything in God's world for you, Demmy. I'd lay down my life for you. You know that." Urged by a sly toe, Pollo's horse sidled closer.

The girl's shoulders lifted in a shrug. "Oh, that! If there's a man on earth who hasn't said that sometime or other, I'd like to meet him. Laying down your life is about the oldest line a man ever handed a woman. I haven't a doubt Adam told Eve that—just before he got a bite of the apple. It didn't keep him from double-crossing her the minute he found he was in bad, you

8

notice."

"Aw, sweetheart! You can't stand me off like this always—"

"I beg your pardon?" Demmy's horse moved aside, leaving a wide space between the two.

Pollo's face darkened. His mouth somehow coarsened, drew down in ugly fashion at the corners. He was not handsome then. "There ain't any law against that, is there? I said it and I didn't stutter. I—" his bold black eyes swung to the Basin beneath them, where the stranger was riding slowly toward the narrow strip of shade which barely reached the trail. "I tell you right now, if I thought that shadow down there really did have a curse in it, I'd haul yuh down there and make yuh own up you love me—or I'd put the curse on yuh for keeps!"

His eyes challenged her and slid away before the look she gave him.

"I ain't crazy," he added sullenly. "But I will be if you keep holdin' me off. I ain't a mouse you can play with. I ain't a kid, either, that you can fool with and forget about. Maybe you can kid the rest of the boys along, and they don't ever forget you're the boss's daughter and they're nothin' but cowhands; but I ain't built that way. I—"

"No, you're not. The other boys understand that a girl can be pleasant and friendly without—" She broke off abruptly, turning to look below.

Her whole expression changed; softened. Her mouth, which had tightened, relaxed into a half-smile. She looked surprised, slightly amused. It was perfectly plain that she had mentally brushed Pollo aside as of no consequence in the face of the pleasing distraction furnished by the man riding along unconscious of their

9

presence (though they were no more than a long revolver shot above him).

Suddenly she threw up a hand, palm outward, toward the man whose awkward importunings had threatened a disagreeable scene. "Listen, Pollo! Did you ever in your life hear anything like that?"

THE SPARK IS STRUCK

DOWN ON CHERRY CREEK TRAIL, riding at ease with his gloved hands clasped one above the other on the saddle horn, Linn Moore passed the sloping point of the bench and saw the Basin spread fair and wide before him like a forgotten Eden yellowed by the late sunlight, with patches of dark brown shade sharply defined upon the high grass.

Since no cattle were allowed in there between April and November, it lay empty to the sky, with no sound save the whisper of a strong southwest breeze, bringing with it a faint tang of the distant prairie fires which gave that deep yellow tinge to the sunlight.

And suddenly, because the scene reminded him of a song and no man is content to ride all day long and never hear the sound of a human voice, Linn threw back his head and burst into the most melodious and utterly unrestrained yodeling ever heard in that valley or in any other. In the Alps, high up on a snow crest where a man stood king of the world for a moment, you might hear the like, but even there the effect would be different: less amazing.

Some sort of plaintive tune went with it, and a more or less casual arrangement of words that could be interrupted at the whim of the singer to let his voice go

10

soaring and swooping in musical scrolls like the
warbling of a flute pressed to the lips of a master.

In the valley—*Yoo-lally-ee-ooo*
There's an echo—*Yoo-lally-ee-ooo*
That brings back sweet mem'ries of you;
Can't you hear it—*Yoo-lally-ee-ooo*
In the twilight—*Yoo-lally-ee-ooo* . . .

Right there, Linn abandoned words and tune
altogether and let himself go. He didn't, very often.
Yodeling he had learned from a Swiss quartet on the
Orpheum circuit, at a time when he had yielded to
urging and his own adventurous spirit and taken his
voice behind the footlights. One season had been more
than enough. In the face of better bookings dangled
before him, he had turned his back on the stage and
returned to the range, where he was more content.

Now, he called yodeling a sort of musical slapstick
singing, a mood gone vocal. It was only once in a blue
moon that he felt that way; never unless he was
absolutely alone with no one within a mile of him.

Just the same, it did limber up a fellow's vocal cords
to cut loose once in a while and *Yoo-lally-ee-ooo* at the
top of his voice. So now Linn yodeled intricately and at
some length, his voice as smooth and effortless as a
meadowlark's song, while he rode at a walk into the
pointing finger of the Black One.

Up on the hill Demmy leaned forward, a hand on her
horse's shoulder, breath drawn in and held while she
listened. Her mouth was smiling, her eyes shone with a
sparkle Pollo had never before seen in them. She looked
as if she had forgotten his existence, as if that stranger
down there had her completely hypnotized with the

11

sound of his voice.

A spasm of fury swept Pollo's face, leaving it ugly and malicious. With a quick sidelong glance at the girl, he let his hand drop back, fingers crooked to close on the holstered gun he carried for chance coyotes.

"Watch me toss a bullet down there in front of that guy," he snorted contemptuously. "I bet I can jar loose a yodel he don't know he's got in him!"

Not quite soon enough, Demmy jerked her horse around. The gun jumped, roaring like an infuriated dog held by the collar. She looked quickly where it had pointed and her face was blank with dismay.

"You fool! Oh, you idiotic moron, you! Of all the crazy stunts for a man to do!"

Down there in the trail Linn had automatically, wheeled his horse and was riding straight up the slope, gun out and shooting as he came. And that, too, was a crazy thing for a man to do—when he didn't know what was behind the bullet that had spatted into the dust six feet ahead of his horse. It was the first instinct that seized him always when danger suddenly confronted him—to ride and meet it more than halfway. So far he had always come out alive and able to call himself a fool when the excitement was over. He had a feeling that he always would. So now he charged the slope. He had fired three shots when he saw it was a girl he was serving notice upon.

He lowered the gun then and shouted angrily up at her, "What's the big idea? You gone crazy, or what?"

It certainly looked like it. For Demmy was reining her wise little sorrel horse this way and that, herding Pollo back from the brow of the hill and blocking any possible second shot from him. It was not until Linn heard a man's voice yelling at her to get back out of the way that he realized it was not the girl herself who had fired.

The hill was steep but his horse made it, heaving itself over the brow with its mouth wide open and panting in loud whispering snorts. Linn pulled up and stared from the girl to the man and back again. "What is this? A range war or something?" he demanded harshly. "If it is, do you have to shoot perfect strangers riding through?"

Demmy looked at Pollo, then back at Linn. "He—We beg your pardon, I'm sure. It was a—an accident, sort of."

"Sort of?" Linn's eyes did not soften.

"Yes. You see, we just rode up here and were looking at the Black One—"

"The which?"

She flung out a hand toward the Basin behind him. "Yes. That shadow down there. You see it, don't you? A monk pointing his finger. The Black One. That's the English for what the Indians called him. It's supposed to be bad luck to ride into that finger—"

"Baloney," growled Pollo, speaking to her and ignoring Linn altogether.

"That's what we were arguing about when you rode along, straight toward the finger. So—"

"So you decided to shoot me and save me from riding into bad luck. Is that the idea?"

A spark was struck in Demmy's eyes. "Something like that, if you insist on putting it so baldly. But you started in yodeling, and Pollo—Mr. Ganzer—just—"

"Say, I'll do my own explaining," Pollo broke in roughly. "I just tossed a bullet down there in the trail to kinda take your mind off your misery. Sounded like you was sufferin' something awful."

Linn stiffened in the saddle. Too angry to feel any

13

embarrassment over his having had an audience, nevertheless the blood rose darkly to his face. The whole thing was astounding. Unless . . .

"You talk like a man who's wintered on the range," he retorted bitingly, "but you act like the rankest kind of a dude. Both of you. Shadows can't give luck good or bad. And out here in the cow country, Mr. Ganzer, we don't shoot at a man unless we mean it. You can't go tossing bullets around just for fun. That's something you'd better learn—and learn it quick; somebody might fail to see the joke, some day. The other fellow will swap lead with you all right—but he'll mean business."

"Well, I can mean business myself, mighty darn quick!" Pollo kicked his horse closer. "Seems to me somebody else was throwin' lead around pretty darn reckless—shootin' at a lady! D'you know you come pretty near—"

Linn shook his head impatiently. "I didn't come a foot nearer than I intended to. When someone takes a shot at me from behind—"

"Why didn't you run?" Demmy asked him suddenly, as if she had just this moment thought of it. "I'm sure that's what Pollo expected."

Her tone was altogether too demure. Linn gave her a swift resentful glance. "I'm afraid that never occurred to me. Dudes wouldn't understand." He flipped his gloved hand up in an involuntary gesture of leave taking and reined his horse sharply away from her toward the Basin.

That perfunctory salute, half-military and half-ironical dismissal, whipped the blood into her cheeks. She held her sorrel in his tracks until Linn's head was down out of sight beyond the rim. They could hear his horse striking hoofs against loose rocks, could hear the

14

gravel rattle down.

Her mortification vented itself in rage against Pollo. "Now," she said furiously when the sounds had diminished until they ceased altogether. "Just why did you fire that insane shot?"

Pollo drew in a breath, leaned and stared full into her eyes. His face was hard and the anger in it had a smoldering look, as if it were not done with the encounter yet.

"You're no dude," she went on. "You haven't that excuse, which it's lucky he took for granted. You know better than to shoot like that unless you've a reason and you're willing to back it up."

Something almost like pain twisted Pollo's mouth and left it again to its sourness. "Oh, I had a reason, all right. And don't think I wouldn't back it up; because I would."

Demmy's eyes widened with astonishment. "A perfect stranger! Why, Pollo? What reason could you have, for heavens' sake?"

For a full minute Pollo resisted her, then shrugged and let his fine shoulders fall slack. He looked somehow heavy and vicious and stubborn.

"It's time we was headin' for home," he said sulkily. "Your maw'll be worryin' about yuh." He lifted the reins and swung his horse around.

"I want to know why you fired that shot. I'm going to stay right here until you tell me, if it's all night."

Already the Basin was filling with dusk. Only the bold top of Shadow Mountain still stood in sunlight, clouds of deep rose and violet behind it. Where they stood the grass had a tint of oranges half-ripened. In Demmy's brown hair the sun found coppery strands and loose hairs that glistened like gold.

15

"Why did you shoot at that man?"

Abruptly Pollo wheeled back to where she held in the uneasy sorrel. He stared at her, squinting through half-shut lids.

"If you'd 'a' seen the look on your face when that damn fool was singin', you'd know." His voice hammered out his meaning, thrust the words at her white-hot with his impotent fury. "And all I'm sorry for is that I didn't shoot to kill!"

MEET LINNELL MOORE

SUPPER WAS HALF OVER when Pollo walked into the mess house. He straddled the bench in the place left for him at the long table, set at the end of the room farthest from the stove where a hanging lamp with a wide tin reflector lighted the cook's bald head to a pale glistening dome. It drew sparkles from the scoured coffeepot which he brought steaming to the table, refilling cups as he made his way to Pollo.

"First time I ever knowed *you* to come last to the feed trough," he jibed, as he took a fresh hold on the handle and steadied the bottom with his apron-covered hand as he poured. "Little more and you'd 'a' been outa luck. What's the matter? Have to walk in?"

Across the table a thin-faced bronc rider with sarcastic lines around his mouth gave a short laugh. "Don't yuh know this is Sunday? Pollo was out on Sunday circle. It was his horse that had to walk in." He laughed again.

"And that's a circle Jim Caplan'll never ride," Pollo retorted. Lifting his glance to grin complacently at Jim, he saw Linn Moore sitting there calmly eating his pie.

16

They eyed each other belligerently.

Then garrulous old Jerry jointed a hospitable fork. "Meet Linnell S. Moore," he said. "Just rode in with a letter of interduction from John's cousin in the bank at Great Falls. F'm now on Linnell's one of the bunch. Linnell, this here's Pollo Ganzer—so called on account of his pretty face, near as I can make out."

Pollo answered Linn's perfunctory nod with a grunt and began filling his plate from the dishes of meat and vegetables carelessly pushed toward him by the others. Linn focused his attention again upon his pie.

Jerry was grinning, showing gaps where both bicuspids were missing from his mouth. Twenty years had creased his kindly face and warped his frame to a permanent bow in legs and back, but in his heart he remained the same loyal Jerry who had rolled a cigarette on the rim of Shadow Mountain Basin while he predicted fat herds for the Triangle J. He talked more than he used to, apparently in the effort to hold the boys together in perfect accord. And since he was also the foreman, he was privileged to say what he pleased.

Now he evidently noticed the hostile stare in Pollo's eyes and tried to talk it down to a more welcoming look. "Near as I could make out from the letter John let me read," he chuckled, "that S in Linnell's name stands for 'sing.' Bob says he's range-bred, all right, but drifted off East or somewheres, and went on the stage, singing. That right, Linnell?"

"Folks call me 'Linn,' Mr. Brown. Yes, I did try it awhile, but it's no life for a cowhand. I've reformed now, and settled down."

Jerry nodded and pointed his fork toward a homely redheaded young fellow with freckles. "So, Red, that guitar of yours'll maybe get some exercise," he grinned

17

again. "Maybe you boys can get together this evening. I sure do love good singing."

Pollo's neck had swelled and reddened. That drooping sullen twist of anger made his mouth ugly again. "Ever try yodelin'?" he asked across the table in a tone which made the other boys look at him.

Linn crossed a knife and fork neatly over a rim of piecrust left on his plate and looked at Pollo, level-eyed.

"Yes, I yodel sometimes—with six-gun accompaniment."

Though he smiled when he said it, the reply was so unexpected and the joke, if it were a joke, was so obscure that Jerry's jaw dropped and let his mouth hang open for a second before he snapped it shut. The other boys glanced curiously from one to the other.

Pollo was speaking arrogantly: "Well, any time you feel like yodeling, just call on me. I'll play yuh the accomp'ament."

"Thanks," drawled Linn, half rising and stepping back over the bench. "But as a rule I like to play my own accompaniment." He pulled a package of cigarettes from his shirt pocket and selected one with negligent attention as he started for the door.

"All right then, we'll make it a duet," Pollo called after him, a forkful of beef pot roast poised halfway between plate and mouth.

"Sure. Any time you say the word," Linn replied over his shoulder, scratching a match on the jamb as he passed through the doorway.

Behind him as he paused outside to get his cigarette going he heard Jerry's protesting voice: "Now, what the hell's biting you, Pollo? What you want to start throwing it into him for? That boy's all right. His folks used to live neighbors to John's cousin over near

18

Lewistown when Linn was a boy. He says he's a fine fellow and a good cowhand. You got no call to start razzing him first thing."

"Aw, he oughta be able to take a joke," Pollo's voice answered with gruff apology.

"Joke, hunh? If that there was a joke, I tell yuh right now it's a damn poor one."

As Linn walked on down toward the corrals he failed to hear what reply Pollo may have made. So here's where that good-looking nitwit hung out, eh? He supposed the girl belonged somewhere in the neighborhood, too. Shooting at him just to see if he would run—well, as Jerry Brown had just declared, it was a damn poor joke. This Pollo might not have any more sense than to do a thing like that, but the girl had looked intelligent . . . Still, if she had any brains, surely she wouldn't have fallen for a sap like Pollo. Just because he was a big handsome brute shouldn't fool a girl with any discernment. Not that it mattered to him, one way or the other. Let it pass.

And pass it did; at least for the time being and so far as anyone save Linn and Pollo could tell. Linn slipped easily into the new environment. Old Jerry acted as if a new phonograph had appeared in the bunkhouse and it must be kept going whenever there was a minute free to enjoy it. Linn liked the old fellow. And since singing was as natural to him as breathing, he never refused when anyone asked him for a song. Moreover, he had the softest, sweetest voice in all northern Montana and the boys speedily came to assume almost a proprietary attitude toward him. Within a week they were calling him "Linnet-sing-Moore" and Linn was laughing over the name.

If Demmy noticed what a musical center the

bunkhouse had suddenly become, she never mentioned the fact nor seemed in the slightest degree interested. Whenever she felt in a musical mood she played her piano loudly with the windows open and sang in a high clear soprano that carried distinctly as far as the corrals if she wanted it to and the wind was right. But never once did she invite the boys up to sit on the porch to eat ice cream in the evening, as she used to do, and never once did she speak of the new man or his voice, even to old Jerry who was like a second father to her.

When Jerry remarked that she just ought to hear Linn Moore sing "Mother Machree," she replied lightly that she had always detested that song and just the night before had been obliged to close the window, because someone was yelping it all over the place. "And furthermore," she added, "once a singing cowboy gets the idea he's popular up here at the house there's simply no getting rid of him. If you'll excuse me, Jerry, I'd rather not start that." (Just what she meant by "that" she did not explain and Jerry did not ask. He let it go and said no more about Linn's singing.)

In that first week Linn learned a good many things about the Triangle J. For instance, he learned that it was frequently called the "Umbrella" outfit, because the brand, a pyramid set upon a long-shank J, much resembled a half-opened umbrella. He learned, too, that the girl's name was Demeter, mispronounced so that Demmy was the natural abbreviation. He thought that was a queer name for a girl, though he did not mention the fact. He learned that she had just finished college last June and was home now to stay; that she was John Coleson's only child and the outfit just about said their prayers to her, figuratively speaking; and that no one considered Pollo's chances with her seriously, because

20

Demmy was just as likely to go riding with Jerry or any other cowboy in the outfit, and did if there was any tangible reason for it and she happened to take the notion. But Pollo took himself very seriously indeed; it didn't take Linn a week to find that out.

Just how Demmy felt toward Pollo he had no means of knowing. As far as he consistently could he kept away from her. And presently his work took care of that problem for him. Within the week, fall roundup began and Linn rode away with the others at dawn, long before Demmy was awake; or so he believed when he looked toward her window and saw the white curtains fluttering gently against the screen as the wind sucked the dotted swiss in and out.

Had he known that Demmy was standing in her pajamas behind those curtains watching the little cavalcade ride away from the corrals, he still would not have suspected that it was an aloof young fellow called Linn Moore who held her gaze until he had ridden over the hill out of sight. He would have taken it for granted that she was staring lonesomely after Pollo, who looked as godlike as his namesake that morning, showing off on a prancing horse as sleek as black satin.

The thought of Demmy Coleson getting up at daybreak to watch Pollo ride off to roundup would have done nothing at all to brighten his day. But however much the girl might interfere with his innermost peace of mind, for the next few months Linn's outer life moved mostly away from the home ranch and was given wholly to the affairs of the Triangle J. Though he did not know it then, that fall and early winter were like a chain: each day a link pulling him inexorably toward the point where, one day, he would be plunged into a tragedy so sinister and mysterious that even the Black

21

One, given all the malevolent power the Indians believed him to possess, must have been satisfied with the trouble that lay under his shadowy hand.

That year had not been kind to the range, nor to the cattle. In the middle of May, when the clouds had hung low and threatened the earth blackly with storms, old Jerry had smiled knowingly.

"Looks like our June rains are coming early, this year," he remarked wisely, squinting around at the moody horizon.

Those May threats were not fulfilled. When the first days of June brought dry winds and hot sunshine, and dust devils whirled like dancing dervishes across the sandy creek bottoms, the Triangle J men lifted their big range hats to mop the perspiration from their damp foreheads, pulled their neckerchiefs over their noses when the dust storms struck, and rode their circles philosophically.

"Guess our June rains are late," old Jerry remarked easily and went his way serene in the belief that nothing untoward could happen to *his* outfit or to *his* range— which was the way he always spoke of them.

But when June passed and brought no rain,—when July came in with fierce sunlight that daily grew fiercer and went out with hot winds that blew a furnace heat across the prairies,—old Jerry grudgingly conceded that this was about the driest year he'd ever known.

Prairie fires started, no one knew how, and ravened over the distant ranges, creeping nearer and nearer to the Triangle J. So far, Jerry's faith was rewarded by immunity from fires. Always some stream balked the flames and turned them back upon themselves, so that they died miserably in charred grass and acrid smoke, starved by their own wanton destruction. Cattle on the

22

farther range lowed complainingly over the black desolation, and clung to the creek bottoms and the coulees that had escaped the fire and had suffered the least from drought.

Then the sheep drifted in like great gray clouds fallen to earth and blown over the hills by a vagrant breeze. Before those clouds the cattle drifted in disgust, their grazing land eaten down to the grass roots, their watering places polluted so that the cattle would go thirsty rather than drink. They lowered horns at the dogs, backed off from creek and spring defiantly, and finally left the coulees and bottomland to the sheep.

That is why the Triangle J went out early to gather their stock. The summer range was bare of feed, and the prairie dogs were digging deep and working frantically overtime to gather what roots they could find and store away underground. And this as all range men know is the sign of a hard winter ahead. Yet the Triangle J felt almost complacent and the cowboys still rode jauntily, work and weather permitting. For the Shadow Mountain Basin held grass in plenty, and neither fire nor sheep had ventured to invade its stronghold.

FIRST WARNING

BY THE MIDDLE OF OCTOBER the last herd was driven into the Basin and Jim Caplan and a fellow named Paddy Blake were placed in charge at the line camp, down near the banks of Cherry Creek, midway between the sandstone walls and bare bluffs at the mouth of the Basin.

It was not a job which any of the boys coveted ; it was too lonely and monotonous a life. Yet Linn was tempted to ask for it just to get away from the home ranch and the close proximity of Demmy Coleson. More and more he was growing to hate tipping his big hat to her when they met, when the thing he really wanted to do was to take her by the shoulders and shake her into friendliness or open quarrel. To watch her smiling and chattering at the rest of the boys and chilling to a haughty formality when he came near was pretty maddening.

He would much prefer a daily ride across the mouth of the Basin to turn back what stock might have strayed beyond its widespread mouth; or an occasional ride back toward the bold base of Shadow Mountain, to inspect the cattle ranging there and make sure no accident had befallen any of them; or even to stay indoors half the day, cooking and washing dishes when it came his turn.

But old Jerry had kept the freckle-faced youth with the guitar on the payroll after the fall work was done, and let an older, steadier man go. He did it, Linn knew, just so that Red could play accompaniments when Linn sang in the long winter evenings ahead of them. To ask for the line-camp job after that would have hurt the old foreman's feelings terribly, and would have been utterly futile anyway.

Linn stayed on and called himself a fool for doing it—especially after Demmy had walked into the mess house one evening just as they had finished supper, waving a legal-looking document for all to see. The smile she gave to Pollo was wholly uncalled for, Linn thought. They were not engaged—nor likely to be, if you could believe old Jerry, who claimed to be able to read Demmy's mind better than she could do it herself.

But it was Jerry to whom she directed most of her

24

remarks. "Meet your new boss! And cast your good eye over this perfectly binding agreement Dad just brought back from town. It's my birthday, you know, and all I get from Dad, it seems, is a half-interest in the Triangle J and all its rights and appurtenances." (Did her glance lift for one second and rest upon a certain young man across the table—the one who was watching her from under his brown eyelashes and trying to appear practically unconscious of her presence? Old Jerry hid a grin under his mustache while he squinted his eyes at Linn, then back at the girl.)

"Well, now, I hope you ain't callin' me an appurtenance," he grumbled, and took the paper from her hand. "A half-interest, ay? I s'pose we can all of us walk chalk f'm now on, or git canned. Bein' a woman I don't s'pose there's any chance of you bein' a silent pardner with your dad, is there?"

"Not a chance in the world!" At last Demmy met Linn's eyes in a brief stare which might have meant almost anything. "Dad's back won't let him ride horseback; you know that. I'm going to learn to handle the Umbrella from now on, Jerry. Dad and Mother want me with them, and I've simply got to have something to do. So Dad says, says he, I may as well learn cattle, since it will all be mine some day. He says you are to take orders from me, Jerry—with him to arbitrate. And—" another swift glance went to Linn before it traveled around the grinning faces of the cowboys— "you'd all better believe you'll have to walk the chalk!"

They joined in her laughter and promised solemnly that they would behave and mind their new boss, and then she was gone again, running up the path with her hair blowing in the cold wind. And life went on just the same, with nothing changed in any particular, so far as

25

Linn could see. Demmy went away on a visit to the Great Falls relatives and was gone—oh, months and months, according to Linn's impression of the dragging weeks; six weeks according to the calendar.

Linn wondered sometimes if she ever mentioned the fact that he was working for her father; for her also, since her birthday. (One of the "appurtenances" made over to her, he told himself with a shrug.) If she did mention his name, he wondered how much Bob Coleson and his wife would tell her about him . . . Not that it mattered in the least. And probably she wouldn't remember anything about that letter of introduction he had brought from Bob Coleson to her dad, or care if she did remember. Pollo was the one she'd be thinking about. Pollo had the looks. That was what counted with a girl.

November brought snow and wind and bitter cold, and the evenings lengthened to interminable hours when the boys expected their tame Linnet to sing, whether he felt like it or not. There was no tangible reason why he should not feel like singing, no reason which he would admit even to himself. Certainly the absence of Demmy Coleson from the ranch could make no possible difference, one way or the other . . .

Nevertheless he rode as often as he could to the line camp, where Paddy and Jim wrangled incessantly and played cards through stormy days to see which one must do the outside chores. He didn't particularly care for either Paddy or Jim, but the ride broke the deadly monotony of the days. So one day he and Billy McElroy rode over to the line camp with the mail and a fresh supply of tobacco. A thin layer of new-fallen snow lay on the ground and the wind drove it in little flurries toward where the sun would rise next morning. It was

26

not a time favorable to keen observation, and Billy rode humped in his big sourdough coat, seeing nothing but the long cold miles he must travel against that bitter wind to reach the smoky warmth of the line-camp cabin. But Linn's eyes were glancing birdlike here and there, deliberately taking notice of every little mark and sign along the trail—chiefly because it distracted his mind from some rather bitter thinking. So he saw something when they crossed a high bare ridge and his gaze clung curiously to the trail.

He had opened his lips to speak of what he saw, when Billy suddenly gave voice to a new worry and Linn let the matter rest for the time being.

"Say, has my nose turned white, Linn?" Billy was anxiously inquiring.

Linn turned in the saddle and squinted critically at Billy. "Well, there's a white streak down the middle, about as wide as the white down the back of a line-back cow," he made careful estimate. "Then that knob on the end is about the color of a hunk of salt pork. Pinch it and see if there's any feeling. If it's numb I guess you better get busy with some snow."

"Oh gosh, I knowed it!" wailed Billy, and leaned from the saddle to scoop up a handful of snow with which he scrubbed his nose vigorously. "I thought I was goin' to get through this winter without freezing my damn face off."

Drawing the frost out of Billy's frozen nose proved an effectual distraction for the rest of the journey. It was not until after supper in the line camp that Linn remembered the thing he had seen which had struck him as being peculiar.

"By the way, boys, have you got a sheep camp up this way somewhere?"

27

"Hope to tell yuh we ain't," Paddy answered with decision. "Haven't saw a sheep since roundup time, thank Gawd. Why? What makes yuh ask that?"

"Well, we crossed the trail of quite a big band, down the river about four or five miles," Linn told him. "The snow was drifting so I couldn't tell much about it, or just how old the signs were, but I know it was sheep, all right."

Billy looked up from his plate in surprise, and Linn chuckled. "It was back there on the ridge where you first began to suspect that proboscis of yours was solid ice. You remember the place. I was going to call your attention to the tracks, but then I forgot about it."

Jim swore. "We didn't ride out south of here yesterday," he observed glumly. "There wasn't any wind and it was cold as blazes. I wasn't feelin' so good, either. And Paddy said—"

"Paddy said nothin'!" that individual cut in defensively. "You was bellyachin' around here like a sick calf and claimed you wasn't able to ride. I shore couldn't be in two places at once. Somebody had to stay in and chop up a pile of wood to run us through the next blizzard. Anyhow, the cattle ain't driftin' much. They're stickin' close to the upper end of the Basin where they git the pertection of the mountain. The feed's good up there this winter, and there's lots of brush down along them spring cricks."

"Paddy's getting so damn fat and lazy he won't make any kind of a ride the same day he chops wood," Jim taunted. "And I sure couldn't of rode a horse yesterday if my life depended on it, the way I was havin' cramps. I must've et—"

"Funny there'd be sheep in that close," broke in Billy, his finger tips gently caressing his purple nose. "You

28

sure you saw sheep signs, Linn?"

"Hell, if there was any signs at all it's a cinch Linn wouldn't pass 'em up," grinned Paddy. "I'll betcha he can tell whether the herder was left-handed or not, and what his dogs' names are. I'll bet he knows what the herder was aimin' to have for his supper, even. How many sheep was there, Linn? You coulda counted the black tracks—"

Linn ignored Paddy, who had a heavy-handed wit that gave him the name among his fellows of being "mouthy." "The signs were there, plain enough, where the snow was blown off the old crust. If you fellows have any doubt about it you might take a jaunt over that way and see for yourselves. Billy couldn't have helped noticing it if he hadn't been all taken up with thawing his nose out."

"Eccleson has been running a band of his sheep off to the south of here," Jim volunteered. "But that's away over the other side of Sand Creek. It wouldn't be them, I wouldn't think. There ain't any feed, even for sheep, between here and there."

"There sure wouldn't be no sheep rangin' on that burnt strip south of here," Paddy declared positively. "Linn musta dreamt he seen sheep tracks."

Linn looked at him briefly, looked away again. What Paddy thought or said was of no consequence whatever. Linn *knew* that he and Billy had' ridden across the trail of sheep where no sheep had any reason to be. He could not understand why they should be up there so close to the Basin. On the bench and even along the creek bottom, a prairie fire had swept the country clean during fall roundup. They must have crossed an eight-mile strip of burned ground, with no good sheep range beyond, since Shadow Mountain Basin lay to the north. To the

29

east of Cherry Creek was nothing but bare range until one passed the point of the mountains, and there were ugly coulees to cross.

No, he could not understand it—and anything that smacked of mystery attracted Linn Moore's interest irresistibly, even though the matter did not in the least concern him. This small mystery did, since it might very well concern the Triangle J.

"It must have been a band that got away from the herder and drifted off their range," Billy hazarded.

"Well, even a cowpuncher ought to know that sheep don't drift against a wind as sharp as we've been having lately," snorted Paddy. Which was perfectly true, even if Paddy did say it.

"Oh, thunder! It don't make any difference to us where they come from or where they was headed for, we ain't herdin' 'em. Dig up your cards, Jim, and we'll play pedro."

"Yes, darn the sheep," Jim agreed. "Paddy'll be harpin' on 'em for a week as it is. You got to have him for a partner, Billy—I'm blamed if I will; it's bad enough to have to batch with him day in and day out."

When they rode away from the line camp next morning, Linn turned diffidently toward Billy. "You may think I'm nutty to be worrying about those sheep, but has it struck you that Eccleson might put a band into the Basin to winter?"

"Hell, no! I should say not. The Basin belongs to the Umbrell', and has for twenty years. You're new in this part of the country, Linn, or you'd know better than that. There ain't nobody would have the nerve to throw stock into the Basin; not even a sheepman."

"I didn't know the Triangle J owned the Basin," Linn admitted. "I thought they only claimed it—which is

30

altogether different."

"No, it ain't a damn bit different. They do claim it—claim it so hard they wouldn't stand for anybody cutting in on the range. A claim that's stood for twenty years oughta be good as a court order. Forget about the sheep. They can't bother us none."

Perhaps that should have reassured Linn, but it did not. The mystery of the thing had caught hold of him and he would not put it out of his mind until he had solved it. "Just the same, I can't help wondering what they were doing up here," he persisted. "I'm going to follow that trail when we come to it, and see where they went."

"Aw, what you want of them sheep? It's going to storm again, sure as shootin'; and I'd just as soon get back to the ranch as not, before she hits. This nose of mine hurts like the devil. I sure don't want to frost it any more."

"You can go on home, Billy," Linn said doggedly. "I'm just curious enough to follow that sheep trail."

But when they came to the place where the trail had crossed, the shifting snow had covered all traces from sight. Search as he would, Linn could find no sign of any sheep. And when they reached the ranch he straightway forgot that such things as mysterious sheep tracks existed. Demmy had come home again—not that it made the slightest difference to Linn.

SHEEP IN THE BASIN

THERE FOLLOWED A WEEK of cold with wind that sometimes reached the proportions of a blizzard. Through blowing snow the sun was trying to shine, one day, when Paddy stamped into the mess house just as the boys were sitting down to dinner. There was frost on Paddy's shaggy eyebrows, frost on the peak of his cap and the collar of his coat. The cold air that swept in with him was like a halo of white steam around his head. A chill draught moved with his great bulk as he passed the table heading for the stove.

"She sure is nippy today," he remarked unnecessarily, pulling off his mittens and tucking them up under his armpit as he spread his thick fingers over the grateful heat.

Old Jerry looked up in mild surprise. He was not expecting anyone in from the line camp, and Paddy was not the type of man to ride out in that weather just for the exercise. He was much more likely to stick close to the cabin and try to scheme some way to do the cooking while the storm lasted, leaving Jim Caplan to take the brunt of the cold. Jerry's mouth was open to ask what was wrong when Paddy turned and met his look.

"Oh, I didn't ride over here for the good of my health," Paddy explained. "I come to tell yuh there's two bands of sheep and a camp, by golly, up in the upper end of the Basin. There's five men and four dogs with 'em, and by the looks they're there to stay. Me and Jim run onto 'em this morning without no warnin'. We give 'em orders to move on out, and they told us to go to hell. I thought maybe I'd better come on over and find out what you wanted to do about it."

Linn looked at Billy and grinned, and Billy pulled his mouth down at the corners in tacit acknowledgment of Linn's perspicacity in insisting that sheep had been driven toward the Basin.

"Who owns the damn things?" Old Jerry demanded truculently, though he was practically certain he knew.

"They belong to Eccleson." Paddy confirmed old Jerry's suspicion. "They're camped right by that upper spring on the crick over to the south, and they've commenced choppin' down them quakin' asps and gettin' out poles to build 'em a shed and corral. They sure picked themselves a fine place for a camp," he finished peevishly, stuffing his mittens into his pocket and turning hungrily toward the table, looking for an empty place.

Old Jerry gave a snort of disgust. "Well," he rapped out indignantly, "I suppose you fellows turned tail and rode off? What'd they do, sic the dogs on you?"

Paddy looked up resentfully from spooning boiled beans on his plate. "They'd've been some dead dogs layin' around there if they had," he boasted sourly. "Jim didn't say much, but I sure as hell told 'em where to head in at. They come right back at me with the remark that they was on Gover'ment land and Eccleson has got as much right to it as anybody. And damn it, we didn't have no comeback to that. That's all Gover'ment land back in there—you can't get away from that fact."

Old Jerry pushed back his plate and got up from the table. Perhaps he was thinking that this situation would have been bound to come sooner or later, and that the Triangle J was fortunate to have been left alone so long. John Coleson had gambled too strongly on being able to hold Shadow Mountain Basin with the two or three claims his riders had located for him down along Cherry Creek. More than one range war had been fought for less cause. He could hope to hold the entire Basin above those claims only so long as the range was plentiful outside. The prairie fires had driven Eccleson to hunt grass wherever it could be found. Look at it as he would, old Jerry must have seen it was a ticklish proposition at best.

He turned querulous. "Seems to me they must have been in there some little time to get all them improvements under way. Strikes me as kinda funny we didn't get word of it before now. I kinda had an idea there was a couple of line riders stationed down there at the mouth of the Basin, that was supposed to wake up and take a look out of the window once every day or two. Fer as I know, John's idee in putting 'em down there wasn't just so they could bake their boots in the oven and punish the grub pile without any interruptions. John's rheumatics is worse today, and I kinda hate to tell him he made a mistake in the men he picked. He sure must of—there ain't no other way that I can see for a band of sheep to get into the Basin and settle down for the winter right under your noses without you fellers knowing a little something about it."

The deep crimson whipped into Paddy's cheeks by the wind could grow no darker. He shifted his feet uncomfortably under the table as if he had expected something of the sort from old Jerry, and was waiting for more. But Jerry only eyed him disgustedly while he picked his teeth with the small blade of his knife.

"Well, I been ridin' all I could," Paddy defended himself sullenly at last. "Jim, he grabs himself a spell of bellyache every time the weather gits bad, and rolls up on his bunk and won't turn a hand. That leaves me with

34

the chores and the cookin' and everything else to do. I didn't ride line when it stormed; the cattle ain't been driftin' down toward Cherry Crick. It's only on nice days when they git to strayin' out into the open, and then I keep an eye on 'em."

He filled his mouth with bread and beans and chewed glumly. "It's over two miles from the cabin to the point of the hill where the trail comes around. With the wind blowin' from the north the way it's been for the last two weeks, I wouldn't smell 'em or hear 'em; not if they kept in close to the hill and sneaked in along the edge of the Basin. I don't know when they done it, but they was cute enough to pick their time."

"They sure wasted a lot of energy trying to slip past you boys," old Jerry retorted. "They could've drove 'em over your doorstep and you wouldn't't've known nothin' about it."

"Point is, they're *there*," Paddy summed up the matter. "It's going to take more'n me and Jim to haze 'em out again. That's what I come to tell yuh." And with that he turned his attention hungrily upon his dinner. He knew old Jerry, and he had no intention of going hungry while he listened to the endless recriminations that would follow. So he helped himself liberally to Irish stew and let the hard words fly past.

"Well, I s'pose I'll have to ride over and see about it myself," Jerry said finally. "Linn, you and Billy better come along. I guess we can persuade 'em to move without much trouble."

Paddy cocked an eyebrow at the implication, and went calmly on with his dinner. "If you'll wait till I finish eatin' I'll go back with yuh," he volunteered as the three began to bundle themselves up in sourdough coats and overshoes for the long cold ride. "I'd kinda

35

like to see the fun."

"Hunh. Yuh lookin' for blood to flow?" flared Jerry. "Yuh better come along and see how easy it is to stampede a bunch of sheepherders."

"You better pack your artillery along, Jerry. There's a fellow they call 'the Fightin' Swede' in the bunch. You ever go up against a Fightin' Swede?"

Old Jerry snorted a wordless contempt of such opposition. "I'll have one of the boys catch up a fresh horse for yuh, to save time. It's a long jaunt over to Eccleson's, and I'll just give yuh the pleasure of escortin' the Fightin' Swede home with his sheep, and taking a message from the Triangle J to his boss. Maybe it might help John's rheumatism some to write down what he thinks of such doin's."

He went out, Linn and Billy at his heels. Between mouthfuls Paddy chuckled to himself and refused to explain just what amused him. As soon as he had eaten he hurried out, still grinning, changed his saddle to a fresh mount, and was ready to go just as the others were starting off. Paddy might look unwieldy as a brown bear but he could move quickly when he wanted to.

They took the trail to the Basin, galloping four abreast until the trail narrowed and grew rough; after that they rode in pairs with Paddy and old Jerry in the lead.

"You used to be able to give a man about all he wanted in the shape of trouble," Linn heard old Jerry observe querulously to Paddy. "Jim's a new man and I don't know how much sand he's got; but what in hell got into you, to let 'em bluff you off? First time I ever knowed yuh to run from a bunch of sheep. You shore must be gettin' old and past your prime."

"Maybe so," Paddy retorted unabashed. "Anyhow,

36

there's gettin' to be too much of me to make a damn target of myself for a man that's hid behind a pile of brush with a rifle. And anyhow," he added, apparently as an afterthought, "I don't go in for collectin' lead. I'm willin' they should keep all their bullets. 'Course, if you hanker after a sample I reckon they'll be willin' enough to accommodate yuh."

"I don't aim to pass up no trades," snapped Jerry. "They pull a gun on yuh?"

"Well, no, they didn't. There wasn't no gunplay made by any of us. We set on our horses and talked polite. But they had us in the open and the Swede had a rifle. Hell would 'a' been a-poppin' if anybody'd made a crooked move.

"No, nobody laid a finger on a gun. How it come about, me and Jim rode up the Basin and poked around through the crick bottoms, lookin' the cattle over. We rode up to about where the eagle's nest is, and was startin' back when I got a whiff of sheep. Uh course, we followed our noses then and located 'em back at that upper spring. They had the band close in to camp and was workin' on a shed when we hove in sight. They've got it about a third done, I should think."

"If they're back up in them quakin' asps why didn't you sneak up on 'em?"

"Only way you could sneak up on that outfit would be to work around close to the cliff on foot, and even then the damn dogs would get wise and raise a ruckus. Nope, you can't do much sneakin' up when there's dogs around. Furthermore they're makin' camp right out at the edge of the aspen grove with that big meadow layin' out in front.

"Me and Jim rode up and asked 'em what they thought they was doin', and they said they thought they

37

was makin' a winter camp, and went right ahead with their work. I started in on 'em polite enough—but I sure wound up profaner than a bullwhacker stuck in the 'dobe. It sure took a heap of cussin' to make them stop their work and take notice of what I was sayin'. They edged over towards a pile of brush and poles, and the Swede had a Winchester in the crook of his arm, but nobody made a move to open up."

"Well, they got to get outa there," old Jerry stated succinctly. "John says he don't want no trouble with Eccleson if he can help it, but just the same he says they got to get out. We may not have no legal right to the hull Basin, but we've shore got what John calls the right of priority. The Triangle J stock has wintered there for twenty years. There shore ain't no room for sheep."

They had entered the Basin and were galloping against a north wind that stung their cheeks and whipped their breath in white steam over their shoulders. Yet overhead the sky was blue and the bright sunlight laid diamond dust upon the snow. Like a great horseshoe around them the bold rocky bluffs walled them in, Shadow Mountain rising bleak before them. Toward it they rode, through scattered bunches of cattle that made way lumberingly as they passed. Once more they were riding close-grouped, four abreast across a natural meadow, and just beyond it in the edge of a grove they could see the unfinished camp of the intruders.

"That there's the Fightin' Swede," Paddy grunted when a big loose-jointed figure came walking out from behind the half-built shed.

Old Jerry nodded. His sandy mustache bristled as he pulled in his lips. He spurred out ahead of the others, who spread a little, just in case real trouble started.

38

"These Eccleson's sheep?" Jerry demanded bluntly.

"Ya-as, dey bane Accleson's sheep," the Swede drawled indifferently.

"Does Eccleson know you've got them in here?" old Jerry's tone boded trouble.

The Swede spat insolently into the snow in front of Jerry. "Meester Accleson choice dis place las' fall for vinter camp. Ay tank he know, all right. Ja, ay tank so." The Swede was grinning impudently.

"Well, you can't run any blamed, stinkin' sheep in here. Pack up your camp and pull outa here as quick as the Lord'll let yuh."

"Ay bane vorking for Meester Accleson," the Swede drawled in his stolid sing-song voice. "Ay don't taking orders from odder mans. Meester Accleson he tall me make vinter camp here on dis place. Ay tank ay go to vork, now." And with that he turned his back square upon old Jerry and his men and returned behind the shed. It was perfectly apparent that so far as the Fighting Swede was concerned, the subject was closed.

It was also plain that the Swede was in charge of the outfit. His two companions who had suspended work to listen to the colloquy turned at his muttered command and disappeared from sight. The visitors might form their own conclusions as to whether they had gone back to work or not.

The three cowboys looked at each other and then turned their eyes inquiringly upon Jerry. Indubitably it was his move.

Jerry sat there a full two minutes sizing up the situation, then wheeled his horse so suddenly that Linn's horse had to back out of his way. "Come on," he ordered them gruffly. They were halfway across the meadow when he turned belligerently upon the grinning

39

Paddy.

"Well, what's so funny?" he demanded. "Think I'm goin' to let 'em stay? You ride over and locate the band that's grazin' north of here. I heard a dog barkin' over that way as we come along. See to it they head for the mouth of the Basin, and haze 'em right along. If you can't handle the herder I'll git somebody that can.

"Billy, you circle around south of here and pick up that other bunch. They're likely grazin' 'em over towards the hill; they ain't east or we'd 've run across 'em. When you find 'em you see they head for home—and if it takes lead to do it, make it count. Only, you want to use good judgment or you'll likely have them three on your back. Don't either of you shoot if you can help. And Linn, you go back and get a couple of men—Pollo and Red if they've come yet with the hay. Bring 'em on over here, and tell 'em to come heeled. Just in case these freaks get bull-headed."

When Linn glanced back over his shoulder, old Jerry was still wagging his head and making emphatic gestures with his free hand, no doubt telling himself what he would do if the Fighting Swede attempted to live up to his name. A great old fellow, Jerry; but past his prime as a foreman.

John Coleson ought to have a son growing up to take hold of the business and run it as it should be run. It did not look as if Coleson would ever be able to ride again, the way his health had broken in the last couple of months. And that girl would never be able to do more than play at running the outfit. Of course, if she should ever marry a real cowhand—but she wouldn't. She'd go for looks; marry some collar-ad like Pollo, all front and no brains. He certainly wasn't the kind of fellow who would take hold and manage the Triangle J. Not in a

40

thousand years. Or it might not be Pollo at all, but some college yap who didn't know a cow from a camel . . .

What they needed was a real manager. Someone whose mind didn't travel in a groove, like old Jerry's. Now that sheep had come into the Basin the outfit was going to find their winter range a problem. They'd have to fight for every bit of it in another year or two, and the fighting couldn't be with guns, either. The time for all that was past. It was going to take diplomacy—probably some kind of compromise. Too bad it had to be sheep.

Linn's mouth drew down at the corners, and to himself he paraphrased sardonically: "Oh, cattle are cattle, and sheep are sheep—and never the two will mix."

Behind these pessimistic meditations on a subject which did not actually concern him at all, Linn's secret, half-conscious thoughts gloomed over another matter which: deny it as much as he pleased, did concern him terribly Demmy. She had been home almost a week now—five days and ten hours, to be exact—and they hadn't spoken ten words to each other. Eight words, by actual count.

It didn't matter, of course—but you would naturally think that after six weeks of gallivanting a girl who had announced herself as the "new boss who was going to learn the business" would at least act human toward the men. Almost a week within shouting distance, and nothing more than a "Oh, hello, Mr. Moore," and "Good morning, Miss Coleson." . . . A fine way to bridge an absence of six weeks! (As is usually the case when a man feels snubbed and slighted without cause, it did not occur to Linn that possibly his own chill politeness had something to do with the girl's manner.)

He had covered nearly half the distance to the ranch

41

and had thought himself into a fine case of the blues when here came three riders galloping down the road: Pollo and Sandy, and a boyish figure he couldn't recognize. Then they surged up, their horses blowing white jets of steam from their nostrils, frost on their chests.

Linn's heart skipped a beat or two. The one he had thought was a boy was Demmy in chaps and sourdough coat, her eyes sparkling with excitement as she reined in close. She lifted a heavily gloved hand and pulled down the masking wool scarf.

"Hello, Linn! Is it true that Eccleson has driven sheep into the Basin?" An odd note of eagerness was in her voice, as if sheep in the Basin were some thrilling surprise furnished for her entertainment. "I could *shake* Jerry for going off without letting me know! What happened? Why are you coming back alone?"

"To get help." Linn felt practically dumb with astonishment.

"Well, it looks as if I had read your mind, doesn't it? I didn't bring all the boys because I wanted to leave someone to do the chores in case we don't get back before dark." She was very brisk and businesslike. She reined in alongside him, waving Pollo and Sandy to the rear. "Now tell me," she said, "just where they are and what they're doing, and all about it."

Amazingly, her manner toward Linn was as casually friendly as if no silent feud had ever existed between them to hold their acquaintance at a deadlock.

42

DEMMY TAKES A HAND

"YOU SHOULDN'T HAVE COME, Miss Coleson. Jerry and the bunch of us can do all that anyone could under the circumstances. It isn't the time for polite parleying, and the ethics of the invasion are largely beside the point just now. The thing we've got to do is run them out of the Basin. There's a big Swede in charge who doesn't seem particularly amenable to reason." Linn was staring straight out between his horse's ears, not looking at her at all. "It may not be exactly pleasant."

"I don't expect it to be pleasant. Lots of things that happen in the cow business are anything else but. I'm used to that. Remember, I've lived here since I was a baby. I've seen and heard things that might surprise you." And she added briskly, "I've got a gun, and I can use it if I have to."

"You won't have to. That isn't what I meant. There may be"—he gave her a quick glance—"language."

"Oh—*that!* Well," she said airily, "I'm a gal of the high ranges, and I long ago learned not to let my right ear listen to what the left ear dismisseth. Language has been bandied about quite frequently in my presence. You should hear Dad sometimes when he gets strung out and going strong." As if lives were at stake she jabbed in her spurs and leaned to the wind, once more masked to her eyes, which shone in slivers of deep blue between her frosted lashes.

Teeth clenched, Linn held the pace beside her. She rode like a cowboy, sitting close in the saddle, legs straight and thrust slightly forward, her weight on the stirrups. Bundled in sheepskin-lined coat with high

43

storm collar, her slim body yet gave to the motions of her horse, blended with it in the easy grace of a rider to whom riding is a natural means of locomotion. He watched her surreptitiously.

As far as that went, Demmy might very well have been secretly studying him also, though apparently she was concerned only with keeping the frost from biting into her face and with holding her horse to his top speed. Linn thought it all foolishness, riding so fast against that bitter wind, and presently he told her so.

"Jerry's waiting till I bring the boys back, Miss Coleson. He won't do a thing till we get there. If you slow down until we're off this bench and down into the Basin, this wind won't be so sharp."

It surprised him a little that she followed his suggestion. After a minute he added, "This thing ought to be settled peaceably if possible. Of course, I don't know how Jerry is in a range dispute, but he was making some pretty wild threats when I left. He may have been just letting off steam. I hope so."

"That's what I wanted to talk to you about," Demmy said astonishingly, slowing her horse to a walk. "Jerry's fine, but he's a regular old fire-eater and always will be. He thinks you can't have a dispute over a range except through gun-smoke. That's partly why I came over. Besides, Cousin Bob says you settled a sheep dispute very nicely once upon a time—"

"Now you listen to me, Demmy," Pollo cut in upon her, spurring his horse up to crowd between the two. "This here's somethin' that's got to be handled right, or you'll have trouble all winter. You've got to put 'em on the run right from the first jump. No use singin' songs to a sheepherder—and that's about as far as this Linnet'll go. What you want," he laughed, "is an eagle that'll
44

make a meal off them sheep."

"We're not sheep-eaters, Pollo. I agree with Linn. I intend to settle this thing peaceably if possible."

"If you have any peace from now on, it'll be because some of us fellas have put the fear of the Lord into them dirty whelps. The Umbrell's spread in that Basin, and she ain't ever goin' to close up; not as long as I've got a gun and can use it."

"Guns," Demmy retorted, "are all right in their place, Pollo, and so are eagles and songbirds and what all. But right now, if you don't mind, I prefer brains."

"And I s'pose you think that lets me out—that the idea?"

"That's beside the point just now. All I'm interested in is getting those sheep out of the Basin and keeping them out without starting a range war. We can't file on all that land, there's too much of it. And we certainly can't let Eccleson go in there and sheep us out. How about it, Linn? That time Cousin Bob told about—was there some special answer you found to the problem?"

Scowling over the snub she had given him, Pollo held up his horse and dropped sulkily back beside Red. They had ridden down off the bleak benchland and were nearing the brush-fringed creek. Here the wind lost force, and down the breeze blowing out of the forbidden Basin the plaintive murmur of sheep came drifting to their ears.

Linn laughed and pointed. "Jerry has found the special answer, wouldn't you say? Here they come, and I'll bet for once in his life Billy's turned sheepherder. The band he went after was over on this side and would come out ahead, I imagine."

"I suppose that does answer the problem for the time being." Demmy pulled down her scarf and rubbed her

45

red cheeks with the back of a gloved hand. She turned in the saddle and looked back. "Oh, Pollo, would you ride over that way and see if Billy's coming with the sheep? If he is, tell him I'd like to talk to him."

Linn eyed the two sharply, wondering what had happened between them. This mistress-and-man tone was something he had never heard before; something wholly unexpected. Pollo's face was black with rage, but he reined his horse savagely toward the sheep and went tearing off as if demons pursued him. Presently, here came Billy grinning from ear to ear, elbows flapping like wings with each lift of his horse galloping toward them.

"Boy, did I haze 'em outa the Basin in a hurry!" he exulted. "And Paddy's comin' with the other band right behind me about a quarter of a mile. Get that darned Swede outa the quakin' asps, and the job's done right now." He looked at Demmy. "Don't you worry a minute, Boss. The Basin ain't goin' to be all stunk up with sheep."

"I'm not worrying. Let's get on up there and have it over with."

But old Jerry, riding toward them from a time-killing inspection of the Triangle J stock while he waited for the boys, had his own ideas about a girl mixing into sheep trouble. He expressed them at some length, but she only laughed in his face and would not listen to a word he said.

"For once in your life, Jerry Brown, you're going to stay in the background and let a woman do the talking," she told him. "All I want of you and the boys is to hang back a little and look fierce. And I'm *not* going to let any of you start a fight. This thing is going to be settled peaceably. You watch."

46

"You can't be peaceable to a Swede," old Jerry retorted glumly.

She shook her head smilingly and rode forward, the five following close and looking altogether disapproving. Before she had come within speaking distance of the new camp the Fighting Swede stepped out into view and stood staring, his rifle at half-aim.

To the gun she paid no attention whatever but rode straight up and stopped before him. "I'm Miss Coleson, half-owner of the Triangle J and speaking for all of us," she said calmly. "I came to tell you that you cannot bring in sheep and make a camp here in this Basin. This happens to be our winter range, and has been for years. I'm sorry, but I'm afraid you'll have to pack up your belongings and find some other location for your camp."

The Fighting Swede gaped at her. "We bane taking order by Meester Accleson," he drawled finally. "Meester Accleson he tall me ve should make camp on 'dis place."

"Mr. Eccleson has nothing whatever to say about the Basin."

"Yust da same, Ay tank Ay vait for orders by Meester Accleson."

Old Jerry suddenly took a hand, pushing his horse in between them. "You ain't going to wait for no orders but what you got. The lady told you to go, didn't she? Now, you *git!*"

But the Swede simply stood there looking stolidly from one to the other. Jerry's hand crept longingly toward his gun, hesitated and dropped to his side. He turned his eyes sidelong toward Demmy, cocking a frost-lined eyebrow like a question mark gone sarcastic.

Demmy straightened her shoulders, her angry eyes fixed upon the Swede. "If you fellows are not packing your outfit in just two minutes—"

Unexpectedly Pollo rode up alongside her. "Two minutes hell! They're goin' right now," he yelled. "Two minutes from now these squareheads'll be halfway home!" And he sent three quick shots into the snow at the Swede's canvas-wrapped feet.

The Swede jumped back, threw up his rifle with lightning swiftness. The click of the hammer going back sounded ominously loud in the momentary silence. To Linn it seemed magnified a thousand times in his brain by the terror that gripped him—for Demmy had charged in ahead of Pollo, straight at that cocked rifle.

"I'LL TAKE CARE OF POLLO"

LINN JUMPED HIS HORSE into the narrow space between them, shouldering Demmy's mount aside and knocking the Swede sprawling on his back in the snow. He leaned and got a grip on her horse's cheek strap, and yanked him around and to one side, out of the mêlée. The rifle had given a strangled roar unlike the sharp bark it should have had, and he looked its way in time to see the barrel flying in one direction and the stock in another, fortunately with no one in their path.

Other details of the picture he recalled later: the Swede on his back with Pollo on top of him fighting like a madman; Billy, Red, old Jerry, holding off the Swede's two companions with their guns, driving them toward the wagon and their makeshift camp.

Demmy was furiously trying to dismount and couldn't because Linn's horse was crowding in too close. Then Linn leaned and caught her, holding her in the saddle.

"You keep out of it." His voice was low, insistent, steadying. "You can't stop it now."

"Yes, I can—I've *got* to. Pollo's crazy. Linn, do something! Pull him off, can't you?" And when he made no move to obey—"All right, if you won't do it, I will!"

"You'll stay right where you are. Let 'em fight it out, now they've started. Even the Swede wouldn't thank me—"

"But I'd thank you. *Stop it,* I tell you!"

"Stop a cyclone!" Linn muttered. But he swung off and gave her his reins to hold. Not that it was necessary, for his horse would stand; but it gave her something to do that would keep her out of harm's way.

He walked over, surveying the thrashing tangle of arms and legs judicially. The Swede had fallen with his head and shoulders downhill over a hummock where an old uprooted tree had left a lump of roots and earth with a hollow behind it; neither a high hump nor a deep hollow, but enough to give Pollo all the advantage. And Pollo was slugging the Swede unmercifully.

Linn waited, saw his chance and yanked Pollo up by the collar. "The boss says quit it. You heard her."

"Leggo. Git to hell outa here!"

"You've licked him; now lay off."

"You take your hands off me or I'll kill yuh!" grunted Pollo, struggling to free himself.

"I'll have something to say about that, old-timer. Get up off him, I tell you."

"Here, what's the trouble?" old Jerry barked, running up. "Swede, you git over to that wagon of yourn and pull out. Your pardners have about got the team hitched

49

up." He stepped toward Pollo. "Here, quit your scrappin', you two!"

"Damn him, I'll kill the sonuva—"

"Cut that out!" snapped Linn, and drove the epithet back with his fist on Pollo's mouth.

With a howl of fury Pollo recovered his balance and lunged forward, but Billy ran up and thrust himself between the two. "Here, you!" he cried reprovingly. "You're getting things mixed. It's the sheepherders we're fightin'! Save your strength!"

But there was no stopping Pollo then. His fighting blood was up, and he had not finished with the Swede and apparently blamed Linn for frustrating his full vengeance. He threw Billy off and came on again, his handsome face transformed into an inhuman mask of savagery. He was throwing off his hampering overcoat . . .

There was just one space of perhaps ten seconds when he was off guard and helpless. And Demmy for the second time rode in ahead of him, herding him back as she would a fighting bull.

"You crazy idiot!" she cried hotly. "If you are bound to fight, at least wait until we've finished the job we came to do. There'll be time enough for you two to settle your argument when we're through with the sheep."

"Damn right we'll settle it! And believe me—"

"Believe me, when I'm through, you'll know you're settled, old boy!"

"Linn, Pollo, stop it!" cried Demmy, almost in tears.

With a shrug of his shoulders Linn turned his back and walked to his horse; and at that moment the Swede, limping off to the wagon, unconsciously broke the tension. "By jiminy, you skoll be planty sorrow on dis!" he bellowed over his shoulder. "Ay skoll tal Meester

50

Accleson. He skoll feex you planty, Ay bet!" And he added a "jiminy" and a string of Swedish epithets that set Demmy laughing.

Even Pollo grinned a little, and Linn chuckled to himself. But a thought sobered him, and he turned to Demmy.

"He'll make a good story, you can bet on that. And the sooner someone sees Eccleson and puts up a squawk about his sending sheep in here, the better chance you'll have of keeping him out. How far is it over to his place?"

He looked from the girl to old Jerry. "I know it isn't my put-in, but if you'll take my advice you'll beat that Swede home and make your war-talk before he tells how this outfit tried to murder him. That'll be his story, you can bank on it."

Jerry pulled icicles off his grizzled mustache while he stared after the Swede. "Well, I was aimin' to see Eccleson—"

"Well, you can just drop your sights a notch and aim at getting those fellows headed out of here," Demmy interrupted him. "I talked things all over with Dad before I left the ranch, and he said I should go and see Eccleson, after I had seen for myself that the sheep were here in the Basin. You don't know it maybe, but Dad foresaw something of the kind after those fires last fall—only he expected it would be cattle crowding in."

"Fur as that goes, I c'n see as fur ahead as anybody," Jerry rasped. "You go over there soft-soapin' old Eccleson, and he'll throw in every band he's got. I know that old coot."

"I don't know anything about soft soap," Demmy retorted. "I know what Dad said to tell Eccleson. He wrote and had Cousin Bob make out an application for a

51

Government lease on this Basin, and Eccleson has no right in here. Of course, the lease hasn't gone through yet—"

"And you're figurin' on tellin' Eccleson that, too, I s'pose!"

"Certainly not. I'm going to bluff him a little. Dad told me just what to say."

"You can't go strammin' away off over to Eccleson's place this time o' day. You had no business comin' over here at all. I've got trouble enough on m' hands without you messin' around. You go on home, Demmy, and tell your Dad I sent yuh."

"You'd better get over there to the wagon and see what's holding up the parade. I'm taking Linn with me, Jerry. You do the bouncing and I'll do the talking. What's Red swearing about?" She signaled Linn to follow and rode away, Pollo staring after her blackly.

Linn hesitated, looking at old Jerry. But that irate old cowpuncher had turned his back and was mounting his horse, mumbling to himself something about "petticoat government." Had he made motions of washing his hands his meaning would have been no plainer. Linn got on his horse and galloped after Demmy.

She heard him coming and held in her horse until he overtook her. She looked at him soberly, a question in her eyes. At that moment one could scarcely have imagined her laughing at Pollo and teasing him for his godlike looks; not Pollo, nor anyone else. Something worried her, Linn thought as he met that look. Something more than sheep in the Basin, though that was cause enough as far as that went.

"I don't want you to think that I'm just playing around at bossing the outfit, or that I'm deliberately taking the reins out of Jerry's hands," she began

52

abruptly as Linn swung in alongside her. "But Jerry's almost seventy years old and he isn't any too strong. And Dad—well, I'm just trying to do what Dad wants me to do."

"Take over the outfit and run it yourself?"

She pressed her lips together and swallowed—but she was a girl, and Linn was nine tenths in love with her whether either of them knew it or not, and she must have felt his interest and sympathy. She looked at him again; looked long because his eyes held her glance. When she looked away her cheeks held a deeper tinge of color.

"Nobody on the ranch knows this, but I'm going to tell you something, Linn. You know when Dad went up to the Falls after me? Well, he went to a specialist." She stopped.

"About his back?"

She nodded. "It isn't his back. He knew it wasn't, all along. At least, he says now that he knew. The back is just a symptom. It's Bright's disease, and pretty well advanced, I'm afraid. So—well, I'm strong as a mule, and fairly intelligent and have no profession, and he wants me to familiarize myself with the business and take over the management as fast as I'm capable."

"No reason in the world why you can't," Linn said, to hearten her. "You've got a loyal bunch of men— including myself—and if any of us can do anything at all—" He stopped, then made another start. "Any help I can give you, you know I'll consider it a privilege to give."

"I—felt that, Linn. I was pretty ornery all fall, but that was just acting up. You knew that. I didn't have anything else to do, I guess. But this—well, Cousin Bob told Dad and me all about you, and how you really were

53

your father's manager until you had a little trouble with your brother—"

"I just licked the whey out of him, if you'll excuse the expression. Then I told Dad I was through, and went into vaudeville for a while—and wound up here."

"Yes, that's what Bob said. Well, he advised Dad to put you in charge of the outfit (I'm laying my cards on the table, as you fellows say). He really made a very strong talk for you, Linn. Your ears certainly must have burned, one evening. And Dad would do it in a minute if it weren't for hurting old Jerry's feelings. You know how he is."

"I know. It would just about kill him if he thought he wasn't the king bee around here."

"That's just it. And we all think the world of Jerry. He and Dad started out as cowboys together, down in Texas. But Jerry drank and gambled and Dad went straight, so—" She waved off further analysis. "So there it is. I told Dad that seeing I really do want to learn the business, perhaps I could persuade you to—well, stand by with the advice, sort of, and let me handle old Jerry. Because really, when you come right down to it, Jerry thinks as much of me, I suppose, as if he were my father."

"I know he does."

"So he'll think he's humoring me along. And if you don't mind—" she became very busy with her scarf, untying it, shaking off the frost of her breath, and fussily retying it again around her collar—"I suppose your help will let you in for a ride now and then with me—"

"And what about Pollo?" A stupid question, Linn told himself, but it popped out before he could throttle it.

But Demmy turned wide, amused eyes upon him. "Oh, Pollo? Why, nothing about him, that I know of.

54

Pollo's very good company, and terribly ornamental, and all that. But as manager of the Triangle J or any other outfit—" She waved off the idea with the graceful turn of her wrist which Linn found so intriguing.

"Why not? How do you know until he tries?" He did not look at her when he said it, however.

Demmy spoke impatiently. "Pollo's mental age is still at the adolescent period. You saw how he tried to settle that little difficulty back there. Fight—that's the only way he knows. I doubt if he ever does grow up, for that matter. And—well, Pollo never managed anything but a bronc, and never will. Dad never even considered him."

"But how are you going to explain—"

"Explain—to Pollo?" Demmy's voice sharpened. "Why in the world should I? I've gone riding with him when he asked me to, but so I have with others. That certainly doesn't give any man the right to explanations."

"I'm afraid Pollo doesn't understand it that way," Linn said dryly, trying to ignore the leap of his pulse.

"No," she said ruefully, "I'm afraid he doesn't. And I'm sorry, because Pollo really is loads of fun, just as one of the boys. But the trouble is that he takes too much for granted. And that's something I simply will not endure, even if I must lacerate his vanity a little teaching him not to take himself so seriously. He's been spoiled, that's all. Too many girls have fallen for that godlike beauty of his, I suppose."

She was talking a little too much about it; protesting too much. And she knew it, evidently, for suddenly she laughed and looked at Linn with shamed eyes that nevertheless held an impish sparkle.

"Oh, you aren't absolutely dumb, I'm afraid," she exclaimed recklessly. "I can guess what you're thinking,

55

and maybe you're partly right. Two years ago, when I came home on vacation and found Pollo hurtling into my startled ken on a flashy brown horse, my maidenly heart turned handsprings and I lay awake nights thinking about his darned eyelashes and that Grecian nose and the perfectly unbelievable curve of his mouth.

"And for a whole month I never spoke to him, I was so afraid I might blush and stammer and tip my hand generally. I called him Apollo (his name is Paul), and when we did finally meet on neutral ground I kidded him unmercifully about his hair and eyes and nose and mouth—"

"And I'll bet he liked it, too."

"He ate it up," Demmy admitted. "It's just possible he sensed my romantic flutterings behind the jibes, or it may have been just his colossal vanity. And the joke of it was that as soon as I got acquainted with him I was cured. Completely and permanently cured. So I never did make a fool of myself really—except in my own secret thoughts. And I've gone on kidding him and trying to keep him from making himself ridiculous."

"You can't," Linn stated, "keep any man from being what he is. Or woman, either," he added, to be fair.

"No, of course not. And I know I'm partly to blame for his possessive attitude. Because I have enjoyed riding alongside a handsome guy like Pollo, more than I have beside Red, for instance, with his freckles and his big mouth, or Jim with a cud of tobacco lumping his cheek like a squirrel hiding a nut—or old Jerry rambling on about his past prowess. It's my fault for indulging myself in a highly decorative escort and trusting him not to overrate my interest." She moved her shoulders pettishly. "In other words, I've been a prize fool."

They rode along the creek trail in complete silence for

56

some minutes, not looking at each other.

"Well, I promise not to overrate your interest in me," Linn said abruptly, grinning in what he hoped was a casual acceptance of the moral.

"That isn't what I'm afraid of." Demmy spoke with impatience. "I've talked pretty frankly, I know. But I've been trying to give you the straight of it, because back there I got a new slant on Pollo. I never thought he was brutal—the violent type. But when I saw him slogging away at that Swede when he was down and couldn't help himself—did you see that savage, brutal look in Pollo's face? Beastly. A—somehow, the look of a sadist. Scarcely human. I—it scared me, sort of. Because I need your help and advice and will have to get it more or less under cover of—well, just riding around together so as not to rouse Jerry's suspicions—" She was floundering again and she was wise enough to stop.

Linn's hand moved involuntarily, wanting to reach out and take hers and hold it. He pushed the offending hand into his pocket and made his voice coldly matter-of-fact.

"I think I know what you have in mind, and I want you to forget it," he said. "Pollo has had it in for me ever since I landed here; since that little encounter over his jocular bullet. And—"

"Do you know what he told me?" Reminded of that incident, she turned and stared straight at Linn. "Just to show you how little sense he has about some things: He said he fired that shot because I was listening to you yodel, and said it was marvelous."

Linn looked away lest his eyes betray him then. "I always knew," he said lightly, "that darned yodeling habit would get me in trouble some day."

57

But Demmy would not be diverted. "A hint of the real Pollo, and I was just too dumb to realize what it meant. But now, after seeing him beat up that Swede, I wish Pollo was in Timbuctoo or some other faraway port; anywhere but here, where he can make trouble."

Before he knew it, Linn's hand had come out of his pocket and closed over Demmy's.

"Don't you worry about Pollo for one minute," he said in a new, vibrant tone. "Because I'll take care of Pollo. He won't bother you if I can help it, and I rather think I can."

There the subject dropped, and the words hung like fog between them afterwards: words neither could brush away.

ONCE MORE THE SHEEP

"WELL, BY THUNDER!" Billy McElroy pointed out across the meadow toward the aspen grove. "What yuh think of that, Linn?"

"Just another job to do over again," Linn answered, pulling his thoughts back from vain speculations concerning the future. "You fellows certainly must be sound sleepers, Jim. Didn't you know you had neighbors again?"

Jim Caplan shifted his cud to the other cheek and grunted. And Pollo, riding sulkily in the rear, muttered into his collar a sentence Jim felt called upon to answer.

"I ain't responsible for the bum job the rest of yuh done yesterday," he said. "Me, I was laid up yesterday with my damn stomach. How'd I know who was comin' or goin' in the dead uh night? What this outfit needs is a camp down at the point of the hill, and a couple more men watchin' the trail. Paddy's so damn lazy he won't stick his nose outa doors b'fore noon, if he does at all. And my stomach's been raisin' cain with me the last coupla weeks. We oughta have help down here, that's what."

"Meantime, there are those darn Swedes, working like beavers mendin' a busted dam," Billy observed while Linn was studying the layout half a mile away.

In that clear air they could be seen laying up poles on the corral which Linn, Billy and Pollo had been sent over to tear down. Jim had joined them halfway down the Basin, saying nothing of any further sight or sound of the sheepmen; yet here they were at work again as if nothing had interrupted their labors. And it was Linn's responsibility today to see that they left. Old Jerry, no doubt prompted to do so, had sent him over to wipe out all traces of sheep in the Basin. Just why he had sent Pollo along Linn did not know, though he could form his own conclusions—which were that both Jerry and Demmy meant to ignore any quarrel between the two in the hope of seeing it patched up somehow. Linn doubted if this would work.

Pollo forced his horse ahead. "By so-and-so, that damn Swede'll go off on three legs this time, or be packed off," he blustered. "We'll smoke 'em out—like we should 'a' done yesterday!"

But Linn overtook him, waved him back. "You heard the orders, Pollo. We're supposed to tear down the shed and corral, but not to tangle with any of the bunch if we happen to meet them. Demmy didn't get to see Eccleson last night. Until someone's had a talk with him we've got to go easy."

"Says you! Think I'm goin' to turn tail and run from that squarehead again?" He reined aside to pass, his face pulled into its ugliest fighting lines.

"Back up. I happen to be in charge of this little expedition. You calm down and stick that gun back in your holster again. You won't need it today."

"You go to the devil. Me, I'm going to finish up what I started yesterday." Anger blazed in Pollo's eyes. That telltale swelling of his neck muscles purpled his face. "Four of us against them three, and you hang back here in the brush stutterin' over what you can do about it! Damn your yellah hide, git outa my way!"

"You stay back here and do as you're told, or I'll go to the ground with you right now!" Linn's own eyes were hot. "Use your head for something more than to give your hat a ride, can't you? Those fellows didn't come back alone—you ought to know that. The sheep are in the Basin somewhere. That's the thing that counts."

"By gosh, that's right," Billy agreed pacifically. "I bet they sneaked right back last night, the minute they seen us ride on home. That'd just be a sample of the gall they got."

"That's about it. We passed both bands this side of Cherry Creek, as we were going to Eccleson's. He wasn't at home and we turned around and came straight on back—though not up this way, of course. We didn't see, hear, or smell a sheep, all the way home. I thought probably they'd taken a shortcut after they crossed the creek. They must have been headed back, though."

"That's the how of it, all right. So now—" Billy looked at Linn to go on from there.

"So now we'll hunt up the sheep and haze them so far they couldn't get back right on our heels if they wanted to. These fellows aren't doing any particular damage— in fact, they're building a pretty good shed. It might come in handy for the outfit sometime, you can't tell." Linn glanced around at the three, trying to keep any rancor out of the look he gave Pollo.

"A c'rell up at this end of the Basin could be used, all right," Jim affirmed.

"So it keeps these jaspers out of mischief, and we'll let them go ahead and work for a while. And we'll get busy on the sheep."

"Now," said Billy, "you're talkin'."

Jim Caplan nodded. Pollo, however, was hot for a fight—guns preferred. He wanted to ride whooping across the meadow and put the fear of the Lord (meaning himself) into the Swede and his fellows. He wanted bullets to fly and blood to flow, and what the aftermath would be for the Triangle J did not concern him at all.

"Aw, have some sense, can't yuh?" Billy exclaimed disgustedly at last. "Dry up and come on. You'll likely get all the fightin' you want, before we're through with this confounded bunch. Save your breath. You're goin' to need it."

Pollo glared, spurred and yanked his horse for spite and looked back at the sheepmen's camp before he turned to follow. "For two cents I'd bounce a rifle bullet off that Swede's dome," he growled; but since no one gave him any further attention he rode on sulking. And no one spoke for the next half-hour.

From a little knoll they sighted a band of sheep, a patch of dirty gray upon the snow. They were moving slowly southward along the bold base of the mountain, and down on the level no Triangle rider would have seen them at all. They were perhaps a mile away—too far for any sound to reach the cowboys halted on the knoll.

61

Linn studied their slow progress for a while. "They're grazing back to camp," he said at last, "and they mean to keep out of sight behind that line of brush. It's funny we didn't see their trail, but with the snow so cut up and trampled from yesterday we couldn't tell much about it. They must have been on the go just about all night, to get away back there." He let his glance move slowly from one to the other.

"Bill, if you and Pollo will beat it on up there and start them down this way, Jim and I will locate the other band. Just as a guess, I'd say they're moving up that draw straight south of here. We'll find them, wherever they are, and head them back down the Basin.

"But now, listen. Whoever gets to the main trail first will hold up the band till the second one comes along. I'm going to throw the two bands together and haze them on across Cherry Creek in one bunch. The herders may miss a meal or two, but I guess they won't starve as long as there are any sheep left. Anyway, it will keep the sonsaguns out of mischief to mix their bands up a little."

"That's the ticket," Bill approved, and rode away grinning. But Pollo's sneer rankled long after the two were out of sight behind an aspen thicket.

For that reason, perhaps, Linn wasted no time on preliminaries when they found the second band of sheep nipping along like a walking gray blanket of prodigious size, coming up the wide grassy draw just where he had expected to find them. With Jim at his heels he rode down upon the herder.

"You turn your sheep around and make tracks out of this Basin as quick as the Lord'll let yuh," he commanded shortly. "And if you don't want a dog shot, make 'em shut up their yapping at us and get busy with

62

the sheep."

The herder, an unkempt bundled figure with a full ten days between his face and a razor, scowled up at Linn where he sat straight and stern in the saddle. "I ain't takin' orders from you," he snarled. "I'm s'posed to graze these sheep up to camp by sundown, and that's where I'm headin'."

Linn's hazel eyes turned almost green as the pupils shrank. Just so the kindliness froze out of his voice. Pollo had heckled him all day in that maddeningly undefinable manner of look and tone and sly innuendo, and now the herder got all the effect. Linn's pent anger exploded in a suppressed fury against the man.

He whipped out his gun and leveled it with grim purpose. "You're taking orders from this," he rasped. "Turn those sheep and head back the way you came."

The herder stared from Linn's face to the gun and back again. His eyes flickered, but he stood his ground in a stubborn silence.

Linn thumbed back the hammer of the gun. "Put your dogs to work and do it quick," he snapped. "Those sheep are going out of this Basin, whether you do or not. You drive them out, or I'll lay you cold and do it myself. You can take your choice—only don't stutter too long."

"SHEEP'S GOT A RIGHT . . ."

GRUDGINGLY THE HERDER GAVE WAY and whistled his dogs to the task, waving his arms in the wide gestures they were trained to obey. "I can drive 'em out," he growled, "but that ain't sayin' they'll stay out. This in here's public land. Sheep's got a right in here as much

63

as cattle. We'll be back—you don't know Eccleson, I guess."

"No, and I don't want to know him. You hustle those dogs and get those sheep moving faster than they are. You've got an appointment down by the creek, and I'm here to see that you're not late. Stir them up—and that means *move!*"

Something in the way Linn fingered his gun must have impressed the herder very forcibly, for he suddenly broke into a volley of shouts and maledictions that sent the dogs scurrying along to the head of the flock. The gray woolly patch wavered, stopped and turned bewilderedly, weazened faces lifted above the press of sheep to stare vacantly with amber eyes, blat a reedy tremolo reproach, and move on. The dogs yelped incessantly along the outer edge, and presently the band was flowing sluggishly down the draw.

Though Linn had expected to be first at the mouth of the Basin and to wait there for the other band, he discovered that the draw wound back and forth across a half-mile width of grassy bottom where the sheep, spreading up over the shallow rim on either side, had grazed along, covering as much mileage as the other flock which had followed a straight line, but keeping well out of sight all the way. Cunning, he told himself, and eyed the herder with more respect for his shrewdness. It betrayed, too, a pretty thorough knowledge of the south half of the Basin—as if this invasion had been long and carefully planned.

Another camp, where the trail entered the Basin, would be almost a necessity if Eccleson persisted. And yet, Linn could not see how that was feasible just now. Paddy and Jim were needed right where they were, to watch a stretch of Cherry Creek where some warm springs, bubbling just under the surface, kept the ground boggy for some distance back, even in the coldest weather. That spot had a great attraction for the cattle, Jerry had told him. A saltiness in the soil they liked, and fencing didn't seem to do much good. Sooner or later they worked through . . .

No, that camp was right where it belonged, in the center of the Basin's mouth and close to the bog. It would take another camp and a couple of men to watch the trail day and night, and no men were available at present. Pollo, Red, Billy, and a fellow they called Big Jack were hauling hay, a hundred tons and more which Coleson had bought down on the river ten miles away, to replace three stacks burned last fall when the fires were raging. The boys would be busy another month at least . . . Before that time had passed, the sheep question would be settled one way or the other.

A confused uproar of four dogs and the reedy plaint of three thousand sheep roused him from his study of the problem—Demmy's problem, which made it vital to Linn . . . The two bands had met and, in spite of the herders who ran and shouted and swore to control their charges and keep them separate, had flowed together, blatting and running here and there in a mincing trot which bounced into a gallop the instant a rider came charging among them.

With whoops and yells and a few shots fired into the air to hasten their flight, the sheep poured out of the Basin. Paddy came loping out from camp to join in the fun, and came near getting a bullet in his face when Jim's horse reared and whirled unexpectedly while Jim was emptying his gun. Instantly the two were facing each other in hot argument, while their horses backed and circled, and the sheep were for the moment left to themselves.

Keeping one eye on the herder, Linn rode over to see what it was all about. Jim, it transpired, carried a double-action Colt of which Paddy disapproved on general principles, as being tricky and unsafe. Paddy believed in thumbing back the hammer before each shot, as holding a man's mind steady on his intent. Their dispute over the relative merits of their guns apparently was but the continuation of an old argument which never would end in agreement, Linn gathered.

"I told yuh times enough you'll blow somebody's brains out with that damn gun!" Paddy shouted as Linn rode up.

"Well, they shore won't be yourn, 'cause you ain't got none," Jim retorted acrimoniously, and turned to Linn. "He claims it's the gun's fault that he got fanned with a bullet just now. He comes fogging up here like a bat outa hell and scared my horse so he stands up and whirls on me—"

"I know. I saw it all."

"Yeah. Well, I was shootin' when my horse swings around, and Paddy's right in line. I like a gun light on the trigger; not too light, but easy. You try 'er yourself, Linn. See what you think of it. I say a man with any brains in his head won't ride up on a man when he's busy shootin'."

Linn fired a shot, reversed the gun, and handed it back, grinning. "A sweet-shooting gun, I'd say. Call it a draw, why don't you, and come on. Paddy wasn't hit— so why all the argument? Wait and settle it tonight, or some other time. Now, you might work off steam on these sheep—"

"I'll shore work some off on Jim, if he don't quit wavin' that damn hair-trigger gun of hisn in my face,"

66

Paddy grumbled.

"Hair-trigger nothin'!" And they were off again, disputing as they rode: two camp partners bored with each other's company and seizing upon the slightest excuse for the interminable bickering that had become a daily habit. Just one way of passing the time, Linn thought as he left them—Jim's high nasal tones declaring angrily:

"She's all right if she's treated right. I wouldn't have a gun like that old howitzer of yourn—take a team of mules to pull the trigger. Any time I git where it's bullets that talks, I want 'em to speak right out in meetin' and no hangin' back. Take a gun like yourn, and the scrap 'd be all over and the cor'ner called in before you got unlimbered."

"And that's as much as you know—" Paddy's bellowing voice came down the wind.

Then Linn was back alongside the scuttling band of sheep and Paddy's heavy sarcasm was drowned in the clamor. Across the lumpy gray expanse rode Pollo and Billy, harrying the other herder before them. Paddy and Jim, no doubt still going strong, hustled up the drag. Here, ten yards in advance of Linn, the herder he was dominating strode with stiff neck and stubborn back, now and then yelling curses at the industrious dogs.

They reached the Cherry Creek crossing, surged over on the snow-crusted ice, moved up the far bank and went on. The sheep were tired out and beginning to mill. The leaders stopped and huddled together, facing the gray army behind them. The four dogs worked like mad, their shrill yelping barks husky with exhaustion. Probably they had been hard at it since daylight, Linn thought . . .

Pity for the animals grew to a sudden revulsion

67

against further coercion. He shouted to Billy, beckoned him back—Pollo too, and Jim and Paddy. They rode up on their sweaty horses and waited for his word.

"I guess this will hold them for a while, boys. They won't back-trail tonight, anyway." He turned to the herder, who was watching him malevolently, his stained teeth showing as his scrubby mustache lifted in a wolfish snarl. "All right, you. I don't care a damn what you do with 'em now, only so you don't bring them back across the creek. That's the deadline for sheep, so write it down in your little book in case you might forget."

"An' now let me tell *you* something! The hull five of yuh, but you music-voice gandershanks in p'ticular: You're five to one, and you've had the drop on me right from the first jump. But if so be you don't git me first, I'll kill yuh for this day's work; any and all of yuh, but you in p'ticular. And don't ever think we won't be back in the Basin, because we will. Eccleson's picked on that fer winter range, and all hell can't keep us out!"

"I think we'll have something to say about that," Linn said hardly. "If you want to wear down a trail traveling into the Basin and back again, that's your lookout, but your sheep won't get fat on it, I can tell you that."

With that parting shot they rode off home feeling fairly well satisfied with the day's work—though Pollo had spells of declaiming what *he* would have done to the Fighting Swede and his companions, the shed, the corral, the sheep, the herders, the dogs, and in fact Eccleson and all his works, if Jerry had been smart enough to put *him* in charge of cleaning out the Basin.

Billy tried his best to shut Pollo up, but without much effect. And though Linn bit his tongue to hold back his resentment, there were some remarks which he could

68

not take in silence and keep his self-respect. So, while the two did not actually come to blows on the way home, trouble was brewing between them, and sooner or later it must explode into action.

Yet the atmosphere at the ranch, when they rode in, made their own quarrel seem trivial to Linn. Bigger issues were at stake here. The clash of property interests had passed beyond the herders and cowboys, and come to headquarters.

Eccleson himself sat upon a huge gray horse at the stable door, and just as they rode up he was shaking a heavily gloved fist under the very nose of John Coleson, who had come down from the house to have it out with the sheepman in the place where, no doubt, he felt most at home: the stable and corrals, which stood for his main interest and ambition in life—his cattle and horses. The old man looked gaunt and ill, his face hollow-eyed and drawn with pain. But he was standing up to Eccleson, his gun hand white-knuckled where it gripped the split-log doorjamb.

"You show me a deed to them fifteen or twenty square miles of land," Eccleson was shouting when Linn rode up and dismounted quietly behind him. "You show me a deed and water rights to all them spring creeks, and I'll keep my sheep off your land. But that land's public. It's open range, and my sheep's got a right in there as much as your cattle has."

"I've got application—"

"Application be damned!" bellowed Eccleson. "You show me the papers and I'll move out my sheep. Till you do, they stay. That's where I stand, and by the lord Harry, that's where I keep on standing!" He brought his fist down on the saddle horn so violently that the gray ducked and snorted.

Linn noticed that, angry as Eccleson was, he brought the horse back with a light rein where most men would have vented their spleen in savage jerking. A man with such superb self-control as that, Linn thought, would be a hard man to beat in a range war. He would fight with his head, and would have every move well planned in advance, just as he must have planned the invasion of the Basin. There would be no wasted effort—and it was to be hoped that he would listen to reason. Still, those fires had charred the range he had counted on, and when a man is fighting for existence . . .

"If you was so dead sure it's open range in there," John Coleson demanded (and he could not keep the querulous tone of habitual suffering from his voice, Linn noticed), "how comes it you've passed it up for more'n five years now, and ranged your sheep all around it without offerin' to push inside?"

Eccleson looked at him almost pityingly, as if the answer were almost too obvious to mention. But he did mention it nevertheless. "I didn't need to push inside. But this winter's different, and I ain't going to see my sheep starve as long as there's a blade of Gover'ment grass to be had. The trouble is, you've been let alone in there so long you think you own the hull Basin. Well, you don't."

"I guess you'll find out it amounts to the same thing," Coleson retorted in a flat, tired tone, as if the altercation were drawing his vital forces from him. "Come right down to it, you don't own the land your home c'rells stand on. But you'd raise hell if we was to drive in a bunch of cattle and take possession." His pale lips worked nervously within his graying beard.

"And that's a blame poor argument. You don't need my c'rells. You wouldn't use 'em if you had 'em. I do

70

need some of that Basin till grass starts in the spring, and I'm going to have it. If you hang onto it, a winter like this, you can be made to sweat for it. Sheep's got a right to free range, same as cattle!" Again his fist came down on the saddle horn.

"I reckon if you had the Basin yourself, you'd take the same stand we do," Coleson retorted, drawing himself up with an unconscious sigh for his aching loins. "We can't let our cattle starve just to make room for your sheep. We need every foot of that range. Why, we're buyin' and haulin' in hay, right now, to feed stock there ain't room for on our winter range! Cows and yearlin's' mostly is all there's room for in there this year—"

"That," said Eccleson grimly, "ain't no skin off my nose. You've been overstockin' the range ever since I moved into the country. It's about time you was sheeped out, the way you been hoggin' the range."

He swept the prosperous-looking spread of corrals and stables with an eagle glance, and turned it sharply upon Coleson at last. "I didn't come over here beggin' favors," he stated harshly. "I come to serve notice. I need some of that Shadow Mountain Basin for winter range. I've got two bands in there that I ain't got feed for anywhere else. They're going to stay. I don't want any trouble—but if it's a case of fight or see my sheep starve, by the lord Harry, I'll fight!"

"Fight it is, then," John Coleson straightened himself to declare, with something of his old vigor. "I aim to do the square thing—always have. But I'm square with my own outfit first. I ain't dealin' out range to you or anybody else till my own stock is fed."

He shifted his feet, took a fresh grip of the slab. "You set on your hind end last fall and let the range burn over

71

this side Cherry Creek, and never sent a man over to help my boys fight fire. We saved the Basin and you never turned a hand. I've got every hoof in there it'll feed, and I can tell yuh right now, we'll have the fun of watchin' our own stock eat that grass." He lifted a fist and shook it.

"So I'm servin' notice on you now, Chris Eccleson: You keep outa Shadow Mountain Basin with your sheep!"

"When you serve notice with a fistful of Gover'ment papers I'll listen, mebbe," Eccleson roared. "I got two thousand sheep in that Basin right now, and by the lord Harry they're goin' t' *stay,* if I have to stand guard over 'em myself with a gun!" With every word of that ultimatum he brought his fist down on the saddle horn like a quick hammer blow.

"You put that in your pipe and smoke on it," he added to clinch his meaning, and wheeled his big gray horse and went galloping off into the shadows that had crept, purple on the snow, to draw the Triangle J and all the rangeland into their chill embrace.

Linn and Billy McElroy exchanged meaning glances, and Pollo turned his head and gave the two a sickly grin. For even he must have wondered uneasily what would happen when Eccleson saw his three thousand sheep huddled in one big band over across Cherry Creek, too hungry and exhausted to travel farther. The war would be on, and it might be a savage one. Probably would be . . .

John Coleson stared at them with his dull, sunken eyes. "Yuh leave them sheep of his in the Basin?" he asked querulously.

Linn's shoulders lifted. "We did not. His sheep are over on his side the creek, all in one big band. We hazed them as far as they could travel. Tomorrow, we can get

72

busy on the big Swede and his pals that are building the shed. We left them alone today— keeping themselves out of mischief. I figured that they wouldn't eat as much grass in a day as the sheep would, and we'd better take the sheep out first."

Coleson's eyes brightened with brief satisfaction. "Eccleson didn't know that, I reckon; about where his sheep was?"

Linn's mouth drew up humorously at the corners. "No, but he'll find it out, I expect, on the way home. And when he does he'll have to buy himself a new saddle. He's just about pounded the horn off that one."

A dry chuckle answered that. Coleson stood away from the support, handling himself slowly as if he were uncertain of his balance. "Keep the damn sheep out if you have to kill 'em to do it. They say the Basin's unlucky—it sure will be, for Eccleson. You better take a coupla men and go stay at the Basin camp, Linn. Do it tomorrow. Come up to the house and we'll lay our plans. And Jerry, you can cut down the hay haulin' one team, and let Billy and Ganzer go with Linn. I'm turning the sheep question over to him to settle."

They were halfway to the house when Linn heard Pollo sneering about folks that would bootlick the old man to stand in with the girl.

IT JUST COULDN'T HAPPEN . . .

ROARING UP FROM THE SOUTHWEST that night, a chinook wind ate the snow from fire-blackened hilltops and sent new streams of water sluicing down the gullies.

73

The Triangle J awoke to find the whooping gale as warm as a breath of spring roistering over the land months ahead of its time.

By daylight the men had eaten and the cook was overhauling stores and piling kettles and pans in a chuck box ready to haul them down to Shadow Mountain Basin, and five bedrolls lay roped and waiting for the wagon to stop at the bunkhouse and pick them up. For Linn had talked long last night with John Coleson and old Jerry, and Demmy had taken a hand in the conference and abetted him in all he advised; and the result was that the hay hauling was to be suspended entirely for a few days and the men all put to guarding the Basin.

"We're due for a chinook any time now," Linn had argued. "In any case you've hay enough to last awhile, and the sheep question should come first. Eccleson's declared war. And right now, the fellow who can put up the hardest fight is the one who will make peace.

"I could take a couple of men down there, and with Jim and Paddy we could probably do a little better than hold our own. Eccleson will probably send in extra men to help those three stand us off at the sheds—or wherever we run across them—and we'll be too busy to keep out the sheep. That's about the way he'll figure, I believe.

"On the other hand, if we go down there in full force we'll handle the sheep and the camp-builders too. They'll think twice about trying it a second time if we make a good job of the first. Five men from here will be plenty, I'm sure. That will leave Jerry and another man here to take care of the ranch chores. I think two or three days ought to clean Eccleson's slate for him and wipe out any idea of using the Basin this winter. And

74

you'll be able to wave your lease or whatever in his face and keep him out. A man or two down there with Paddy and Jim will be enough, after the first big session—and I don't expect any bloodshed," he added, smiling across at Demmy. "Not half as much as if we went at them short-handed."

"In that case,"—Demmy instantly seized upon his statement,—"you can count one more. I'll go along and help drive sheep."

There had been a good deal of argument over that, and when he went to saddle his horse after breakfast Linn still did not know whether Demmy had been serious or not. He hoped not. It was no job for a girl; and moreover, Pollo was in one of his mean, sneering moods and there was more than a slight prospect that he and Pollo would fight it out before the day was over; they had nearly come to blows at breakfast.

He was just looping up the latigo when here came a black horse galloping up the road, a drunkenly swaying figure on his back. Linn left his horse and ran out to get a better view, past the corner of the corral. Pollo, who was already mounted, rode out to meet the horseman.

"It's Paddy!" he shouted over his shoulder, and took down his rope to catch the horse, it was so plain the animal was not under control of its rider. He came back leading them both straight to where a little knot of the boys had gathered waiting.

Paddy it was, without a doubt—but a Paddy more dead than alive, judging from the look of him. He sat slumped in the saddle like a loose bag of meal, his hands clenched upon the horn, his head lolling upon his chest. Linn ran to his side and caught him as he toppled off when the horse stopped abruptly, bridle reins flopping loosely below its neck.

75

As he pulled the half-conscious man off, he felt his palm press into something sticky and warm. Linn's face went hard as iron.

"Paddy's shot, boys. Take him, some of you."

It was old Jerry's arms that eased Paddy to the steaming ground, Sandy and Billy eager to help. Linn ran to his horse, thrust toe into stirrup, and leg over cantle seemingly in one motion before he turned, reining close to the group, and peered down at the limp and bleeding figure in Jerry's arms.

"What happened, Paddy? Can you tell? Did the Swede's outfit jump Red and Jack? They were sent down to the Swede's camp before daylight to watch it—not to start a fight."

Paddy struggled to lift himself, wagging his head loosely as he stared blankly in the direction of Linn's voice.

"No—" He tried to raise his lolling head. "Jim—in the cabin—shot—" He flapped a hand, trying to point toward the Basin. His head dropped and his eyes closed in a faint.

Linn straightened and sent a quick glance around the group, making lightning-quick plans.

"Billy—you help get Paddy inside, and then you and Pollo head for the Swede's camp and see what happened to the boys. If they aren't there, come on down to camp; if they are, better let 'em alone. Sandy, you come along with me. I'm going to Jim." He turned, saw Pollo wheeling his horse to ride off. "Hey, Pollo! You're to go with Bill—"

"Go to hell! Jim's a friend uh mine!" Pollo yelled defiance, and spurred his horse to a run. After him raced Linn.

Fast as he rode he kept turning the disaster over in his

mind, trying to picture for himself just how the killing—or at least the shooting—had come about. There certainly wasn't much mystery in the beginning of it, he thought. It was the sheepmen, of course. Either Eccleson had found his sheep on the way home and had gone straight to the camp, or the Fighting Swede and his fellows had taken action when night came and the sheep had failed to come blatting into camp.

The Swede would probably have done just that, but somehow Linn could not picture Chris Eccleson turning aside to ride several miles to a line camp and shoot it out with two men in the night. Why, so far as distance was concerned, the home ranch was nearer.

Well, he might have gone to the Basin to see what had happened to the men left there at work. He'd be anxious, of course, and the herders wouldn't be able to tell him anything about it. But to go on down in the night and shoot Paddy and Jim didn't seem logical, somehow. Not like Eccleson as he had read the man . . .

Still, the old man had said he'd fight to keep his sheep in the Basin; Linn wondered if this was what he called fighting. Why, yesterday, when they had stopped in the brush across the meadow and seen the Swede and his helpers at work, it would have been the easiest thing in the world to pick them off with their rifles. It would have been plain murder, of course; but so, thought Linn, was this murder—if Jim was dead.

Shot, Paddy had said; but shot too badly to make the ride into camp, or he never would have let Paddy come with that bullet wound in his side. Say what you would, Jim Caplan wasn't yellow. He had nerve, that boy. He'd go out fighting if he went at all. How Paddy ever had made it in to the ranch was the mystery—and the only one, really.

Or so Linn thought then, as he tore across the soaked black burnt-over ground on the bench, trying his best to overtake Pollo.

But Pollo always rode good horses. He would scheme and wheedle and trade around with the boys, getting the best and the showiest in his string. He certainly had picked a good one this morning to ride; try as Linn would, Pollo kept the lead and even gained a little on the level, and he was nearly a half-mile ahead when they went galloping into the Basin and up the creek to the thin grove of cottonwoods in the hollow where the line camp squatted.

As he neared the dip of the Basin to this shallow depression, Linn looked back and saw two other riders coming not more than a mile behind him. Then he rode down into the hollow out of sight, slowed, and made the rest of the way with his panting horse at a walk. No use riding into a bullet if you can help it by using a little common sense, he thought. He nearly yelled again at Pollo, who was flinging himself off his horse and bolting inside. The fool . . .

Linn left the trail and circled the hollow warily, trying to pick up strange tracks in the fast-melting slush-snow. But the softening snow blurred what marks there were, and he could not take time to make any careful search. He was peering into the bushes beyond the corral, toward the sheepmen's camp, when the muffled roar of a six-shooter came from within the cabin.

Instantly he wheeled his horse back that way, rode up within easy shooting distance of the door, jumped off, and stood behind his horse, watching the cabin. He was not more than fifteen feet away—far enough to have a clear view of stable, corral, and the bushes behind, yet close enough to hear what went on. He waited.

Nothing happened; no other shot, no sound of voice or of heavy bodies flung this way and that in combat. He could see the door, and one square window set in the end. Another, at the back, was out of sight; but it was small and high and he would have heard any movement there, so he felt satisfied that he had the cabin covered.

But no one showed at door or window. There was no sound save Pollo's horse rolling the cricket in his bit with his tongue, reins dropped to the slushy snow. Strange that Pollo wasn't yelling and blustering . . . That absolute silence within the cabin wasn't right.

"Pollo!" Linn shouted impulsively. "Pollo, what's happened?" And suddenly he ran to the cabin, flung open the door and went in, the acrid reek of gun smoke filling his nostrils as he went in. Finger on trigger, he flattened himself against the wall until his eyes accustomed themselves to the semi-gloom of the place. Then he saw.

Never, so long as Linn had memory left to him, would he be able to forget what he saw: Pollo lying on the floor, half on his side, one big-roweled spur clogged with his horse's blood and hair, the other caught on a ragged edge of the gray blanket on Jim's bunk; Pollo with his Greek-god face frozen in a look of utter amazement, his bold black eyes staring up at the ridgepole as if something there astonished him; Pollo dead, with a reddish stain over his heart, a viscid red pool beginning to widen on the grimy floor just under his left shoulder.

And ten feet away from him on the bunk, head slumped down on his right arm, hand still gripping his gun as if he had indeed gone out fighting, Jim Caplan, dead and staring impersonally toward the door with his glassy eyes . . . Dead and cold . . . Linn reached out and

79

touched his face, felt it stiff under his fingers, shuddered, and withdrew his hand.

And the silence in that room was terrible; a creeping deadly thing, punctuated horridly, emphasized but not broken by the loud incessant ticking of a cheap alarm clock hanging by its buckskin thong from a nail beside the wavery little mirror over the washbench next to the door.

Save for Linn and those two dead men, the cabin was empty of anything in human form—anything save the meager furnishings, the tiered bunks along the back wall, one with Paddy's tumbled blankets . . . No long search was needed to prove that. And he had been watching the door and the window . . .

Incredulously he bent again over Pollo. The man was dead, no doubt of that; already his eyes had the glazed empty look. His gun was in his holster. He had rushed in headlong to see what had happened to Jim—and Jim was dead and already stiffening, and Pollo was dead with a bullet in his heart.

It just couldn't happen that way. But it had happened nevertheless. That shot had been fired inside the cabin. The smoke proved that . . .

Linn shook his head, turned, and went out, his gun hanging loosely at his side.

WHO SHOT POLLO?

DOWN INTO THE HOLLOW galloped Sandy and old Jerry, snow clods hurled from the trail as the shod hoofs lifted and shook them off. One small hard ball struck Linn on the leg with a smart blow as they pulled up before him, but he never felt it. His gun was still in his hand, forgotten.

"Is Jim—?" Old Jerry began, breaking off the question. Instead he asked, "Where's Pollo at?"

Linn looked at him as if he did not understand. Then he pointed a thumb over his shoulder. They would have to be told, of course. But the thing was so utterly impossible . . .

"Jim's dead. Been dead for hours." After all, why mention the unbelievable? Let them see for themselves, he thought.

Old Jerry swore a shocked and meaningless oath as the two swung off their horses. Mechanically Linn moved aside to let them pass, followed them inside, and stood against the wall. He was still too incredulous to reason about this thing or to form any theory at all.

"Good—*God!*" gasped Jerry, whispering the last word. Sandy said nothing. They stood there frozen, eyes bulging with amazement. " 'S he—dead?" Jerry gasped again in an awed whisper.

Linn said nothing, because there was nothing to say. And Sandy slowly turned and looked at him, his gaze moving from Linn's stony face to rest upon his right hand.

"Lemme see that gun," he said quietly—too quietly.

With a surprised glance into which understanding flashed in the next instant, Linn proffered the gun, butt first. Old Jerry stirred, eyed the two with a grim interest, but he did not say anything at all. He simply watched while Sandy, a tall and silent Scot, pulled off his gloves and felt the gun barrel with bare fingers for the warmth of a shot; lifted the muzzle and smelled it, pulled out his handkerchief and twisted a corner to thrust into the barrel and test for oil. He got it. He inspected the cylinder, found it full.

81

"Hunh!" he grunted then, and passed the gun to Jerry for a like examination.

He stooped and had to turn Pollo's body a little to get at the holstered gun, but for the moment he did not touch it. Instead he looked up at Jerry who was turning Linn's gun over and over in his hands.

"When ye finish with that one," Sandy said in his flat expressionless tone, "I'd like for ye to mind close when I take out Ganzer's for inspection."

"Sure." Jerry turned his bewildered stare upon Pollo. "Linn never done it. His gun's clean."

"That," said Sandy, "we've yet to make sure of. It could be managed—" He broke off, signed to Jerry, and rolled Pollo's body again. "Ye'll notice the gun is settled in its holster. He had made no move to draw—or it could be that the gun was put back."

Again he sniffed and held the gun barrel in his fingers, whirled the cylinder and tested for oil (the boys had held an informal gun cleaning bee in the bunkhouse the night before in anticipation of trouble this day). Pollo's gun was clean and fully loaded.

Sandy made sure of that and saw to it that the dazed Jerry was certain also. He stood up, pushed his hat forward, and scratched the back of his head where the hair was thick and kinked with black woolly curls, staring down at the dead man in deep thought. Rousing himself, his gaze went from window to window. Both had broken panes, and the front window had a round hole with shatter-rays out from it marking the path a bullet had taken.

Linn's eyes followed his glance. "I was in sight of that window from the minute he came in till I followed," he offered. "I think you'll find that hole was made from inside."

82

Sandy nodded, his little, birdlike brown eyes studying Linn's face. "And what about that one?" He tilted his head slightly toward the back window.

"That one I couldn't see, but I was close all the time. I think I'd have heard anyone there. I didn't hear a thing but the shot." And he added, "We can easily find out."

He led the way out and around the cabin to the window, Sandy and old Jerry close at his heels. At the back the cabin was set up a foot or more off the ground, which there began its slope to the creek. Inside, the window was nearly shoulder high to a man of average height; out here . . .

"It would take a tall man to do it from here," said Linn. "I could, or you—or the big Swede up at the sheep camp; but a man would have to stand right under the window to pull down on anyone inside."

With one thought the three dropped their gaze to the ground just beneath the window, dimpled with the drip from the eaves and with no other mark upon it. Yet their own boots had picked up clayey soil, their own tracks were printed deep behind them. They stepped close (though keeping to one side) and looked in the window—first Sandy, then Linn, and last of the three old Jerry, needing to crane his neck a little.

They saw Pollo curled on his side as he had fallen, one foot tangled in the dragged blanket off Jim's bunk where the spur rowel had hooked in the tear. They saw Jim lying there with the fighting snarl on his face, his gun clenched in his hand.

They stood back and looked down the bare and sodden slope where the chinook was gnawing away at the remains of snowdrifts lodged against rocks and old logs. They turned and eyed the empty corral, and the stable with Jim's horse peering out the opening toward them, blazed head and rough brown neck thrust through.

"It beats all hell," said old Jerry as they turned back to the door. "I just can't believe it." For once his garrulity had dried to terseness. It was big Sandy, an old and steady hand with the outfit (though he could not have been over forty) who took the initiative as a matter of course.

He stopped inside the door and looked at Linn, their eyes nearly on a level. "What happened? You're the only one can tell." Except for the faint tang of Scotch, his voice was as before expressionless.

Linn's head moved in a slow denial. "I don't know what happened. I was close, but I don't know much more than you do. Pollo was ahead of me all the way—"

"We could see that much," old Jerry grunted. "Look at them spurs. I told him times enough to cut out tearin' the hide off his horses with them spurs—"

A shiver caught Linn, passed, and left him curiously calm. "Yes, you've told him times enough," he said softly. "He won't cut another horse up with the spurs."

"You and him," Sandy stated heavily, "had bad blood between ye . . . 'Tis well known ye started off in the mind to fight; the both of ye. Ordinarily . . ." The roll of his *r's* gave the word a sinister import.

"Ordinarily, you'd say I shot him, and I couldn't blame you. But I didn't, as it happens. Pollo beat me here, piled off and rushed inside, and the door slammed behind him. I didn't follow him in right away. I rode over toward the corral and scouted around a little for tracks, or some sign of the sheepmen cached in the brush . . .

"Not long—not more than a minute or so. And I didn't get out of sight of the cabin at all. I was anxious about Jim, of course, but Pollo was with him and I just

84

swung aside and took a look in case there was somebody waiting to dry-gulch us."

Sandy nodded. Jerry said, "Common horse sense. Poor business to go bustin' in—"

"I heard the shot. In the cabin here. So I jumped my horse over this way where I could stop anyone who came boiling out, and got behind my horse and waited a minute. I'll take you out and show you the tracks, over behind my horse. There's a snow bank there. I stood right beside it."

"We'll look," nodded Sandy, though he did not move.

"Well, I didn't hear anything more. Nothing at all. Not even the sound of any fight, or any talking. No one showed up outside. It seemed so damned queer I yelled to Pollo. That didn't raise anybody, so I came in." He spread his hands in a gesture embracing the scene at which they were gazing. "I couldn't make anything of it, any more than you can. So I went outside to have a look around, and you came."

"It sounds reasonable," Sandy admitted judicially. He tilted his big hat forward again over his wide strong nose, scratched his dark curly pate meditatively. "But if it was that way, *who shot Pollo?*"

Old Jerry snorted, stirred himself to action, dropping the look of old age as he stepped grimly to the bunk and laid his hand upon Jim's gun hand. Over his shoulder he looked at Sandy.

"If you're thinking this gun could have been used on Pollo and put back again, come and see for yourself. Jim's got it in the grip of death and his hand's stiff. He was shootin' when he went out, I reckon."

"I was thinking of that very thing," said Sandy, and stood beside Jerry to test the remote possibility. He shook his head in tacit dismissal. "The gun could be

85

forced from his hand," he stated in that judicial tone he assumed when making a positive statement. "That could be done. And it could be put back. But unless I am mistaken the fingers wouldna grip that hard once their hold was broken—" His little sharp eyes sought Linn's face for confirmation.

"I think you're right, Sandy." Linn went and felt the iron grip of Jim's dead hand. With the two watching him, he even lifted the hand and attempted to release the gun without breaking back the fingers. "The way they're hooked in the trigger guard and clenched tight together—no, it couldn't be done. I'd bank on that."

Sandy gave him a queer look. Linn met it fairly, his eyes bright and hard.

"You can judge for yourselves. You needn't take my opinion. Form your own conclusions."

Sandy turned and walked to the rear window, stood for a minute looking out. Linn saw what he saw: the brown steaming slope to the nearest point of brush, fifty yards of bare open ground which a man must cross before he could gain the most meager shelter. There were places where a dog could not have run without leaving his footprints plainly stamped in the soft snow lying all honeycombed by the devouring warm wind from the Gulf Stream far to the southwest; between the drifts was the soft wet soil, spotted here and there with tufts of weeds.

"It couldn't have been done from the outside unless a man turned humming bird and hovered before the window long enough to shoot," Linn summed up the impossibility, breaking a bewildered silence. "Even a man on the roof would have to be an acrobat and a trick shot as well—and he wouldn't have been on the roof in the first place."

86

Sandy turned heavily back to the room. "Then how would ye say it was done?"

"I don't know, I tell you. It was the sheepherders—I'm sure of that. I don't know how—" He swept the bare log walls with a slow seeking glance; the table with a few dishes and condiments grouped in the center (sugar in a tomato can, salt in a milk can, pepperbox, a bottle of ketchup and a can of syrup, teaspoons, and a dish of stewed prunes). Suddenly he went down on one knee, pushed back his hat, and peered under the bunks while the others watched him in silence.

He got up shaking his head. "I just happened to think that no one looked under there," he explained. "Boys, I'll stake my life that no one came out of this cabin after Pollo went in. I was too close, the two or three minutes I stayed to look around, and I was never out of sight of the door. If Jim had been alive and out of his head, he could have mistaken Pollo for someone else and shot him as he came in . . ."

He flung out a hand in a helpless kind of way. "But Jim's been dead for hours. Before Paddy left here, probably."

Old Jerry nodded confirmation. "Three, four hours, I'd say. Takes over two hours to stiffen up a corpse—closer to three, accordin' to what I've saw. Musta been right along about daylight when Jim cashed in. Hunh, Sandy?"

Sandy looked at the clock. "It's now half-past nine. It's daylight about six. It would have been then or soon after, I'm thinking."

"So that lets Jim out, naturally. And whatever you two may hold in the back of your minds about me, I haven't got that possibility in mine. I *know* I didn't shoot Pollo. I know I was a good fifty yards from the

87

cabin, over toward the stable when the shot was fired. I *know* that door didn't open till I opened it myself to go in. Then the powder smoke boiled out in my face—and the only gun in the cabin besides Pollo's, which was in its holster just as you found it, was Jim's empty one gripped in his hand.

"So there you are. You've got the whole layout just as I saw it first. All you haven't got is my own certainty that Pollo was dead when I came in here. He was shot in this cabin and there's got to be a way for somebody to shoot him. One of the sheepmen—unless you think I—"

Old Jerry reached out and slapped a hand down on Linn's arm. "Nobody believes you done it, son. Me, I know damn well yuh never."

"Thanks. You know Pollo and I never did hit it off together. I admit I never liked him—but I'd give my right leg to have him alive right now."

Sandy cast an oblique glance toward him and went on twisting the end of his black mustache. "Ye mind we've three men less than we had yesterday, and we'd none too many then to keep yon sheep on the run. 'Twould be a poor time to settle private quarrels when the outfit's being pulled into a sheep war."

"You're damn right. And I'm the one Mr. Coleson put in charge of the sheep war, as you call it. We're doing no good here now, boys. It's as Sandy says, we're three men short right now, and the fellow who did this can't be far off. I wish, Sandy, you'd ride out and see if you can pick up his trail leaving the Basin. If it's one of the herders we hazed out yesterday, he'd have to get back to his sheep. Don't see how it could be one of them, but we've got to know where the sheep are and which way they're headed this morning.

"Jerry, now you're down here, how about going with

88

me up to see how the boys are making out up at the sheep camp? We may be able to pick up a trail—we can, if this is the Swede's work."

"You're damn tootin' I want to see that Swede again!" snarled Jerry. "Killin' our men off without a dog's chance to save theirselves—c'm on, and le's go."

At the door Linn paused to take one more disbelieving look at the two silent figures they were leaving behind: Jim with his face fixed in a snarling grin as if he had just pulled the trigger and made a hit that pleased him; Pollo lying with his cruel spur caught in Jim's blanket, his velvety black eyes glazed and staring astonished at the roof.

With a cold weight in his chest he went out, then, and showed the two where he had stood behind his horse in that minute after the shot when he watched the cabin. They mounted and rode away, each man scanning the ground, looking for the tracks of the killer—looking, but finding no trace.

FIRE DOES IT

LONG BEFORE THEY ARRIVED in sight of the sheep camp the howling chinook wind brought the intermittent sound of gunshots. Linn's mouth tightened at the barking explosions which told only too clearly that the day's fighting was far from being ended. He was not by nature a fighter; he had talked last night optimistically of what Demmy had called armed peace: a show of force so implacable it would discourage Eccleson at the start. And here was war forced upon the Triangle J in spite of itself, with three men already lost.

He rode around the meadow, toward the nearest point

where rifles cracked. And presently he came upon Billy McElroy standing behind a tree watching the camp, his six-shooter in his hand. Behind him old Jerry ducked deeper into the brush as a shot came from the shed. The bullet whined past Linn and smacked into a tree.

Billy made a flapping motion with his free hand, imploring Linn to get out of range. "What you tryin' to do, make a collection of lead?" he expostulated. "Here's the rest of us been layin' low ever since we come, and you amble out in plain sight. Boy, that Swede's out for bear, now I'm tellin' yuh!"

Linn rode up to him and dismounted, the deep gravity in his face making him seem more deliberate than he was. He went up and stood beside Jerry, a tree between himself and the shed.

"Are all three in camp, Billy? Or don't you know?"

Billy gave him a quick look and a sardonic grin. "You stick around awhile and you'll think they're all there! Sure, they are. Why?"

That question got no answer then. Instead, "Where are Jack and Red? Do they know whether all three have been in camp all the time?"

Understanding flashed into Billy's eyes. "I getcha, Linn. Yeah, Red and Jack have been peckin' away at 'em about all the time since they come. I asked 'em about that, first thing. How's Jim?"

Linn told him in one word how Jim was, and Billy swore a shocked and commiserating oath. "It wasn't either one of these birds done it," he said, looking from Linn to old Jerry, who had come up to them afoot. "Red told me they've been peckin' away at each other ever since they got here, just about—and they've got all the best of it so far. Better location and all. I told the boys about Paddy and Jim gettin' shot, and they say it couldn't be any of these; must be one of them herders sneaked back, don't yuh think?"

"They got Pollo, too, whoever it is," old Jerry announced bluntly. "Shot 'im in the cabin right under Linn's nose, as yuh might say. Got clean off without bein' seen. And he didn't leave no tracks. Hell of a note when yuh can't even get a line on the thus-and-so that done it!"

"Pollo?" Billy turned one shoulder against the tree and stared from one to the other, his eyes resting finally on Linn's face. "You and him was together—and you say you never even saw the man that done it?"

"There wasn't any man." Linn's tone was resentful, as he realized how foolish the truth sounded. But he went on doggedly in the faint hope that Billy's brain might fix upon the answer to the riddle. "There wasn't a soul in the cabin. Jim was dead on the bunk with his gun in his hand—dead long before we got there. The shot that killed Pollo was fired inside the cabin; I opened the door and the smoke boiled out at me, so that much I know for a fact. Three facts, and if you can find the other one you've got me beaten . . ."

"Three? You mean—"

"The cabin was full of gun smoke; Pollo was dead and there wasn't a living soul anywhere around—except myself, of course."

Billy's eyes averted themselves from Linn's face. "Oh," he said, and slowly an embarrassed look came into his face. He flushed and turned to peer intently toward the camp; muttered something about "that damned Swede," and fired a shot in his general direction without taking any careful aim.

Suddenly his face cleared. Relief showed in his eyes when he looked at Linn. "Pollo shot himself," he declared. "You had me goin' in circles, there for a minute, but it's plain enough now, come to think of it. Mebbe he done it right then so's it would look like you' done it. I wouldn't put it past him."

"No, he didn't. His gun was in its holster and hadn't been fired. Jerry can tell you that. So now what do you think?" Sandy's doubt of him Linn could accept as a foregone conclusion. Sandy was of the dour disbelieving type. But Billy was as warm a friend as he had in the outfit, other than old Jerry; he felt the immediate, pressing need of knowing just where Billy was going to stand.

But Billy had pulled himself together and refused to be tagged as friend or doubter just then, it would seem. "Looks like the Injuns was right, wouldn't yuh say? Prob'bly it was that damn Shadow." Then abruptly he threw off his manner of evasion. "Hell, Linn, I don't know no more'n you do," he said frankly, "except it wasn't any of these jaspers. Not unless miracles is happenin' here too. These fellers have been poppin' away with three guns ever since I come, and you can see for yourself, a jackrabbit couldn't leave camp or git to it without us seein' it." He shook his head. "Nope, you'll have to look down the other way, towards Eccleson's, I reckon."

"Sandy headed over there. Well, this checks up with our not seeing any tracks coming up this way, then."

"Here comes the boys," grunted old Jerry. "Mebbe they'll have somethin' to say that'll help."

Red and Jack came crouching behind the thick clumps of brush, wanting to know the latest news. They got it—from Billy, who repeated almost word for word what Linn had told him, except that he rather stressed the uncanniness of the killing.

92

"Now, what do yuh think about a thing like that happening in this day and age of the world?" he propounded when the recapitulation was complete.

What they thought only they themselves could know. What they said was considerable, though it did not help any. They had arrived to find the sheepmen working by the light of a bonfire—all three of them. There had been the expected exchange of unpleasantries, together with some shots. Since that time, which was before daylight, no one had left camp.

They puzzled over the mystery, much as Billy had done, and it struck Linn curiously that the very fact that Pollo's death was unexplainable pulled it into the foreground and made it of more importance in their minds than the shooting of Jim and Paddy. He realized that they were more or less accustomed to the thought of sudden death by the bullet trail. Even though the land was considered pretty well tamed, this section was rather remote from the world of paved streets and police stations. Men still settled their quarrels out of court more often than with the aid of lawyers, and gun fights were not so uncommon as they should have been; though murder would not go unpunished, once they were certain it had been done.

But to have a man shot down by some invisible means in a cabin as bare of hiding places as that line camp—that was something different. That called for discussion and even argument. Squatting on their heels there among the trees, they had old Jerry map out the scene with a stick on the ground, and say just how Pollo lay when they found him. With that fixed in their minds, they considered this window and that, quizzing Linn as to just how sure he was that he did not take his eyes off the door. They did not seem to realize that any time had

93

elapsed between Linn's arrival and old Jerry's . . .

It was one of those interludes not to be explained except by granting human nature certain twists of mood. Red had one theory, Jack another, and each tried to convince his listeners that it could have happened that way. The fact that two men with whom they had eaten and bunked and spent long hours in the saddle lay dead a half-hour's ride down the Basin was for the moment set aside; the manner of their death became paramount—especially of the death of Pollo.

It was the Fighting Swede himself who put a stop to theorizing and brought them back to the siege. He appeared suddenly between the shed and the tent, flapping a dish towel in his left hand while he held his gun in the right.

"Ay bane like for know vot you fallers vant to do," he shouted, advancing toward them. "If you skall set on talk all day, I go for make dinner, by golly. Ve bane pratty busy, und skall not vait for fighting more."

"Well, by thunder!" Billy ejaculated, and laughed.

Linn was on his way to meet the Swede. Here, at least, was something tangible; something simple and understandable. "You needn't wait for fighting or anything else," he said quietly. "You've got to leave this Basin, and you may as well do it now, without any more waiting."

"Ay do not going. Meester Accleson—"

"Eccleson's got nothing to say about this. It's what we say that goes, around here. Either you go peaceably, or we'll have to put you out. Get that straight in your head. We don't want to fight, but we will if we have to. So make up your mind, because if we do have to start in on you fellows, there won't be any more of this pea-shooting. I can tell you that."

The Swede eyed him stolidly. "Val," he considered, "Ay bane vorking for Meester Accleson and ay skall earn my monies, you bat. Ay don' be vaisting time. Ay tank ay skall make dinner now." And with that he turned his back and went into the tent, not deigning another glance in their direction.

Big Jack swore a vicious oath. Billy answered that with a mirthless laugh.

"Yeah, I guess we'd all like to lay a bullet between his shoulder blades," he observed feelingly. "I never thought much of these guys that'll shoot a man in the back—but I can sure see the point right now."

"That squarehead's goin' to take a lot of killin' before we're through with 'im," Red prophesied gloomily. "Well, you're s'posed to be the boss now, Linn. You going to let that hunk of spoiled tripe get away with it?"

Linn finished lighting a cigarette before he answered that challenge. When he did he knew exactly what he was going to do. There was a new and purposeful gleam in his eyes, a squaring of his shoulders that made even old Jerry look at him attentively.

"Back down this little ridge here, a couple of hundred yards, maybe, I saw a down tree that looked to be two-thirds pitch. We'll crawl on our horses and ride off down that way—and if you've got anything on your minds you'd like to tell our friend the Swede, you might do that too as you ride off. Just give him to understand that there's another day coming.

"We'll load up with pitch, all we can pack. Bring it up that little draw there and leave the horses, and then sneak up behind that shed and lay the pitch and brush where it will do the most good. While they're 'making' dinner and eating it, we ought to be able to get the shed going good. Let's go!"

They grinned and made for their horses, mounted, and rode boldly out in full view of the camp. Linn reined over toward the tent.

"Hurry up with that dinner, and then pack up and leave this Basin!" he shouted. "This is the last notice you'll get, so I advise you to get under way. We're through talking."

Three unkempt heads appeared like jack-in-the-boxes in the tent opening. Three rough voices raised ribald shouts of defiance, following the Triangle J riders until they had crossed the meadow out of sight.

"I thought of some more I wanted to say, Billy mourned as they circled back to the pitch pine log. "Damn it, Linn, you'd oughta waited till I'd got it wrote down. You know I can't think and talk at the same time—"

A little of the weight lifted off Linn with the laugh he gave to Billy. "Well, I only hope they can't think and eat at the same time," he remarked, as he kicked pitch knots loose from the rotted wood. "I'd hate to have the Swede get to wondering why we pulled out all of a sudden. Try and get lots of splinters and knots, boys, so we can scatter them along the two walls out of sight. Those green logs are going to need a lot of heat to start them off, but once they're blazing the whole thing will go like a prairie fire. The thing to do is start the fire in several places simultaneously."

"Yeah, and all at the same time, too. I getcha," Red elaborated enthusiastically. "That's the stuff, all right."

Whereupon Billy snorted, caught Linn's eye and winked. Trivial as it was, the little byplay helped bring him back to normal. For the moment he could forget those two dead men down there in the cabin. He went about briskly gathering wood into a bundle which he could bind with his rope and drag up the gully.

"This time we go through with the job," he told them when they started back. "They've started the killing. If it comes to gun fighting, hunt cover and make every shot count. Maybe we can put it over without that; I hope so. But if we can't—remember Jim and Pollo and Paddy."

"You're damn' right," growled old Jerry, who had maintained a glum silence, looking older even than his years and seeming glad to shift the leadership to younger shoulders. "It's fight f'm now on. We been too damn' easy, just like I told yuh."

Linn nodded acquiescence and led the way back to within a few hundred feet of the shed, where they tied the horses, well under cover.

"Better get the stuff ready to light," he said. "Just shave up a stick of the richest pitch—we'll each set a fire—and make it good and hot. Thank the Lord this wind will fan it up so they'll never put out the fires once they start. When you get 'er going, take cover and keep everyone away from it—if you have to drop him in his tracks."

While he talked he was whittling pitch, the others following his example.

"I'll take that farthest corner," he went on, gathering an armful of wood. "The rest of you scatter out, and be sure she's going good before you leave." He lifted his head to squint down across the gully. "See that clump of brush and rocks right across over there? We'd better get in there, I think. Each man can watch his own fire, and we'll command the whole situation."

"Yeah, and have the drop on 'em, too," Red supplemented as gravely as before.

"That's the idea. Are you ready, boys? Then come
97

on—let's go."

Each with his armload of pitch-pine, they ran through the water-soaked snow that had been drifted onto the edge of the small gully, racing to see which would be first—and to get through and back before they were discovered. The pitchy shavings flamed with a hot aromatic smell of resin. As quickly as they piled sticks crisscross against the log wall, the avid flames licked them with long yellow tongues. Black oily smoke rose like signals that were whipped away on the roaring wind.

When the crackle was likely to reach the ears of the men inside the tent, Linn waved the cowboys back and they scurried down across the little gully to the shelter he had chosen. In panting silence they stood there, watching the five small fires climb and go creeping along the aspen logs to form a wall of flame.

SET AFOOT

Two minutes—three—passed while they stood there watching. Then the wind grew sportive and with a gusty whoop it lifted the tallest flames and folded them around the poles and brush, just that day laid in the roof, ready for the thick covering of dirt.

"All hell can't stop 'er now," gloated Billy as the fire roared across the roof, feeding on the tangle of dry twigs and branches.

A yell from the tent drew their eyes that way, as the Fighting Swede came charging outside bellowing like an enraged bull. Close behind him came the two others, crowding to be first through the tent opening. Gun in hand, the Swede stopped and stared around him, peering

98

intently down across the meadow where he had last seen the cowboys. Plainly his slow brain held him there bewildered, unable to grasp the full import of the disaster or how it could have been accomplished.

He called something in Swedish to the two at his elbow and dashed toward the burning shed, though he must have known he took the risk of being shot down as he ran; or perhaps he did not care just then. When the others did not follow, he glanced back over his shoulder and swore a jumble of English oaths and what must have been his mother tongue, his arms flailing as if he were fighting wasps.

Irrepressibly, Billy stood up laughing derisively. "Yah—ay tank so, by yiminy!" he shouted, and caught Linn's warning scowl. "Aw, he knows we're around somewhere," he defended his boyishness. "You didn't mean for us to lay here till dark and never make a move, did yuh?"

With a surprising swiftness the Swede whirled and fired, and a bullet plucked at the left sleeve of Billy's coat just opposite his heart. Billy's look of astonishment would have been comic at another time, though now Linn saw nothing amusing in it.

"You would play the fool and try and get a bullet in you," he said shortly, and stepped out in full view, his gun aimed straight at the Swede's big body, no more than eighty feet or so away.

"Put up your hands!" he ordered, as harshly as that melodious voice of his could speak. "You know you're whipped."

For answer the Swede fired—and another gun, a little to the right of Linn, barked savagely. It sounded as if the two shots synchronized exactly, but that could not be so, for the Swede's shot went far to one side as his arm jerked with the impact of a bullet through the biceps.

"Darn you, Linn, get back here!" Billy yelled at him anxiously. "Come on, boys! If Linn's goin' to commit suicide—get them two squareheads and I'll take this big stiff for a cleanin'." He glared at Linn as he went by: "A hell of a boss you are—go make a target of yourself first thing—"

Linn shouted at them without avail. They were gone, vanished behind the swirling smoke. The fight shifted without warning, with the sheepmen behind the burning shed, rushing out unexpectedly to fire and ducking back before anyone could take aim. At least the Fighting Swede made two successful rushes; the other two Linn did not see; though, from the shooting the cowboys did, he judged the three were in sight at least part of the time.

The green logs burned with dense smoke which the wind forced down along the ground for seconds at a time, obscuring the view completely until a gust lifted the acrid curtain and bore it away across the meadow. During one such interval Linn saw Red sitting on the ground shaking his head like a drunken man who refuses to get up and go home. The others had disappeared.

With his heart beating in his throat, he ran over there and got the homely young guitar player by the shoulders.

"Red—you hit? Where you hurt?" Then he saw blood dripping down into his collar, the side of his head smeared with it.

Red gave his head a final shake and looked up. "Lost a piece of m'right ear somewheres around here," he muttered lugubriously. "Don't know where in thunder it

100

went to."

Though it wasn't really funny, Linn laughed from sheer relief and left him there. The fight again had moved on, past the burning sheds. The Swede was using his left hand and his aim, manifestly, was not exact, though he kept firing back at the Triangle J men as he retreated slowly into the brush. Then he too disappeared, where it was evident his companions had fled before him.

Nothing there for Linn to do. He turned back, went on to the tent and busied himself for a minute or two. When he came out again flame tongues were licking hungrily up the dirty canvas. He went over to where Billy was standing behind a bush, staring blankly past the shed. Billy looked at Linn and pointed.

"I'd swear that Swede was right there, by that dead tree, two seconds ago," he said disgustedly. "The tree ain't big enough to hide a snake. I can't see where he went to—just when I was sure I had him cornered, as yuh might say. For a feller as big as he is he sure can get outa sight quick!"

"I touched a match to their tent," Linn told him, tilting his head that way. "No use dragging things out. If we don't clean camp today we'll be fighting off and on all winter." And then, "Where's Jerry?"

Billy sent a questing glance around. "They was over there a minute ago, tryin' to get 'em a woolly-back. But this darn smoke's so thick, right when you pull down on a man—and they sure are hard to hit, boy! I never seen such dodgin' in m'life. That damn Swede, now!"—he harked back to his grievance—"They're all scattered in the brush."

Linn went to the corner of the shed, peered cautiously down beyond it, then made his way boldly to where the

101

fire had been started. With the wind blowing heat and smoke off the other way he could take stock of the damage and study the sloppy snow beyond for tracks. There were many, coming and going from the gully; too many to have been made altogether by themselves. Those of the Fighting Swede showed plainly in the watery snow, huge as the spoor of an elephant. In spite of Billy's protesting oaths, Linn followed that trail to where it suddenly ended at a patch of bare ground ten feet from a thick clump of brush.

"He made a long jump here," he called over his shoulder to Billy. "The smoke settled in here—I remember it now. It hid him long enough to let him take a running jump into the brush. Pretty cute. He probably lit running." He turned back, grinning at the other. "Well, our main object is accomplished, Bill. We came here to put that darned Swede on the run, and we have. If they try to come back they're bigger fools than I take them to be. They'll have to start at grass-roots and build them another camp—and I don't think they'll try that in a hurry."

"Them? They'll try anything. All I wanted was one more crack at that big ox."

Off to the left, toward the meadow, there rose the sound of six-shooters popping, and the enraged shouts of Jack and old Jerry, followed by the crackling sound of men forcing their way at a run through brush.

"Something's wrong down there." Linn started running toward the noise, Billy at his heels. There was a final burst of shots, the thud of rapid hoof beats, and nothing more save the snapping of brush and the two men cursing at the top of their voices.

Then big Jack burst into view, panting, his face purple with rage. When he saw Linn he swerved toward

102

him in another spurt of speed.

"They stole our horses!" he yelled jerkily, adding epithets as well not repeated here. Slowly, he gathered breath for details as old Jerry came wheezing into view. "We seen 'em run down into the gully, and me an' Jerry took in after 'em—but the so-and-so's got 'em a horse apiece and was gone 'fore we could draw a bead on 'em in the brush."

"I'll bet that's what he jabbered to 'em back there when they come outa the tent and he seen we had 'em cold," mourned Billy.

"I know—and it's my fault. I should have left a guard with the horses. But they were pretty well hidden, and tied so they couldn't be stampeded, and short-handed as we are we just had to take a chance." He flung out a hand impatiently and gazed around the crestfallen little group. "Like a damn fool, I thought they'd try and protect their camp, so I stayed back above the sheds and tried to keep an eye on the gully from there. But the smoke was thick—"

"That's what give 'em all the advantage," old Jerry said sourly. "They took damn good care to git behind that smoke. I never did git a fair shot a tone of 'em."

"Their tent caught fire—" Jack cried unnecessarily, pointing at the collapsed and smoking camp.

"I set it afire," Linn said shortly. "Scatter out, boys, and see if we can't locate their wagon and team. They didn't move back in here afoot, that's certain. We'll have to get down to the line camp and rustle a horse or two—"

"Damn right," old Jerry agreed. But his shrewd, smoke-reddened eyes rested commiseratingly upon Linn, as if he saw the Shadow fall again upon his face.

Linn looked at him, looked away. "Let's go," he said,

and started down across the meadow, leaving the burning camp behind them.

IT WASN'T THE HERDERS

BY TAKING SHORT CUTS that they would scarcely have followed on horseback, the small ridges and gullies they crossed were so steep, they straggled dejectedly down the last sloshy slope to the line camp about noon. And there Linn halted old Jerry and pointed to fresh tracks in the soft soil.

"Somebody's been here and gone again within the last half-hour," he said. "Sandy, do you suppose?"

"Might be. Went on up where he thought we was, I s'pose. We prob'ly missed each other. We could, easy, if he follered the trail—and a-course he would."

"That's what we should have done, I suppose. I seem to be piling up blunders today. I wanted to save time, and now we'll have to stick here till Sandy comes back and we hear what he's got to report."

"Don't ever think we can't use the time to good purpose," Billy put in with studied cheerfulness. "Me, I'm holler as a coon tree right now—" He bit off the whimsical complaint, Linn knew, because he had suddenly remembered what they would find in that cabin.

Billy's next words proved Linn's guess was correct. "Say, we can carry the boys out into that old shed, can't we? Or do you s'pose we'll have to go through all the red tape of havin' a cor'ner monkey around here?"

Old Jerry's face twitched. He lifted a gloved fist and dropped it again. "Long as we bin in this country there ain't no cor'ner ever come nosin' around the Triangle

104

J," he rasped. "Nor no sheriffs either. We've had our little troubles, too—I ain't sayin' things has always went along peaceful. But them folks is put in office to see to it justice is done by all. They got their hands full without us pilin' our own little troubles on 'em."

"You mean this isn't going to be reported?" Linn was surprised and showed it.

"Not till we find out who done it. When we git our hands on the killer it'll be time enough to call in the sheriff—mebbe. We aim," said old Jerry sententiously, "to save the county expenses. The sheriff understands all that. Years back he rode for the outfit. He ain't goin' to come snoopin' out here unless we send for 'im, and he knows damn good an' well that if we do give'im the high-sign he better come a-runnin', 'cause it'll sure be serious.

"No," he added, as they approached the door, "we can go ahead and bury these boys, soon as we git around to it, and then go ahead and settle the sheep question. Then'll be plenty time to size things up and see whether it's goin' to be worth Joe Ellis's time to git on the job.

Linn unconsciously slowed his steps, holding Jerry back for the moment. "I didn't know the old order still held good over here. What about the rest of the townfolks : the district attorney, for instance, and public opinion?"

Old Jerry paused long enough to give him a sternly reproachful look. "Hell, we're law-abidin' folks and they know it. They mind their own business and let us mind ours. Always have, and I guess the rule ain't goin' to be busted yet. When we git the killer, then it's time to talk."

It was the Old West speaking, and Linn seriously doubted its authority, but he did not take up the argument then. As Jerry said, there would be time later to talk.

In a curious silence the three who had not seen what lay inside went in. A change, slight though it was, struck Linn like a blow. They had left the dead men exactly as they found them, too shocked and in too much haste to find the killer to think then of small conventions. Now, each man was covered from head to feet with blankets pulled off Paddy's bunk—as if Sandy had not wanted to look again into those eyes that looked with that blind fixed stare and saw nothing.

It wasn't much. It was a small friendly gesture, which any man would do except when under such stress as they had been before. Yet it affected Linn strangely just at first, hammering home the stark reality of death in that room. Then Billy and Jack removed the blankets and they all stood looking, taking in every detail, seeing that Jim's gun was empty, that Pollo's was in its holster, clean and carrying its six loaded cartridges.

It was too much for Linn. Abruptly he whirled and went out and down to the stable, stepping around puddles of snow water in the uneven path. Pollo's horse, hastily turned into the corral with the bridle off when he and Jerry had left for the sheep camp, walked to the fence and watched him with big wondering eyes. His scored flanks showed rusty streaks of dried blood matted in the hair . . .

Linn looked and glanced away frowning. Pollo had been no more than a big handsome brute of a man, utterly vain, a braggart, and a bully. Had he gone out in less mysterious fashion his going would not have caused more than the passing regret one feels for any life snuffed out. But to have him go as he had gone—to hear the shot, to be within easy calling distance, and yet to know absolutely nothing of the manner of his going—left one with a prickling of the scalp and a chill sick feeling of horror. It just wasn't natural; there was something devilish about the whole thing, as if something beyond death had met him inside the cabin and struck him down.

In the stable Jim Caplan's horse whinnied coaxingly, and Linn opened the door and went in and talked to him in the low caressing tone men use to dogs and horses when their mood is friendly. The deep-chested gray was twitchy, nervous as a broncho, though he wanted the petting and the murmuring voice soothing while the strong dexterous hands patted and rubbed.

Jim's horse—and Jim was dead; and his saddle hanging by one stirrup on the log wall behind the door would hang and rot, and be chewed by rats, and the lining be moth-eaten, if it must wait for Jim's hands to lift it down. Linn thought of that and a lump rose in his throat so that his voice was husky and he fell silent. Though Jim Caplan and he had never been more than casually friendly, his eyes could shine with unshed tears for this hard-bitten rider. Jim had gone out fighting; died when he had emptied his gun . . .

A thought struck Linn and made him gulp. Why hadn't Jim left his mark on his assailant? Whoever it was had gotten away and left no trace of blood behind him. It occurred to him that, had he not seen Pollo enter the cabin long after Jim had died, those two dead men would have told a plain story of a more or less ordinary gunfight.

As it was, Pollo explained nothing, not even himself. But Jim had died understandably, at any rate, with a bullet in his left side and one just under his Adam's apple which must have severed the spinal cord and killed him instantly. He had at least had the satisfaction of fighting back as long as a beat was left in his bold heart.

But Pollo didn't have a chance to fight. His hand that was always too ready to reach for his gun was not given time even to move toward it before he dropped. He must have been dead when he hit the floor; the position of his body showed that. If he still lived and could look back upon that empty shell he had occupied, that unwarned death must be the bitterest knowledge he was taking away with him. Somehow that was the horror of it for Linn.

With slow unthinking movements he saddled the gray, ready to ride to the ranch with news of this fresh tragedy, and to bring back horses for the boys. But though he did not own it to himself he loitered in the stable, giving the boys time enough to carry those two out into the shed before he went in. There was too much to do, too much to think of now. He couldn't afford to let his nerves and his imagination hold a wake together over the dead . . .

Sandy was riding down into the hollow as Linn led out the gray. He hastened his stride and reached the cabin just as Sandy swung down off his exhausted mount, that stood with head drooping and legs braced to hold up its tired body. Sandy and Linn looked at each other questioningly, as if each believed the other would have vital information to give.

Together they reached the door and went in. Then Linn broke the silence between them—a silence that had also fallen on the others when they entered.

"Well, what did you find?"

Sandy's eyes went to Jim's bunk, now stripped of bedding, to the floor still wet from a vigorous scrubbing with cold water and a broom. He looked up, met Linn's eyes, and nodded toward the spot where Pollo had lain.

"It wasna' the herders, one or both," he stated in his slow monotonous voice with its tang of Scotch. "I rode down the creek and across it, following the trail of the sheep where you drove them. The two bands you threw together yesterday have not been separated, and the two men and four dogs are workin' them back this way. The grass is fed down to the roots where they are, but they're hunting such bits as they overlooked before, and comin' slow.

"Both herders are afoot with no horse in sight, nor any sign of one, and to get to this cabin and back again before I arrived they would need to fly. I rode on till I met Eccleson himself, coming with two men. It couldna be any of them, for I saw them coming over the ridge five miles and more away before we met, and I was then beyond Black Coulee."

Old Jerry got out his pipe and tobacco pouch and prepared for a leisurely smoke. "Well, that bein' the case," he observed to Linn, "you sure are welcome to go ahead and boss the job, for all me. Things is comin' too thick for me, I can tell yuh those." He glanced at Sandy, whose sharp black eyes fixed questioningly upon him. "Them three up the Basin never done it, either," he explained.

Linn thought of another small mystery that had been teasing at his mind like a lone mosquito humming over one's head in the dark.

"Sandy, was it you came back and—covered Pollo and Jim with blankets?"

Old Jerry whirled, stared from one to the other with his mouth half-open. Apparently the strangeness of that small ceremony had passed unnoticed until now.

109

Sandy's bushy black eyebrows pulled together. "I rode away when you did, and I came back the same. I havena been near this cabin since we left together, until now. Blankets over them, ye say?"

In the startled silence the cowboys looked at one another. Linn's jaw lumped along the sides as he swung toward the door. "We left them just as they lay. When we rode up half an hour or so ago and came in, they were covered with blankets. There's something fishy going on here, and I'm going to find out . . ."

He was gone, the sentence unfinished. With a common impulse the rest followed, leaving the cabin empty and silent save for the snapping of the fire someone had started in the stove.

"I'M HELL ON WHEELS . . ."

LIKE HOUNDS AT FAULT on a cold trail they worked divergently from the door, trying to pick up some trace or track not left by one of themselves. That warm strong wind had bared the ground save where drifts had packed against some rock or bush, and whatever imprints had been made in the snow were gone as completely as the intelligence from the eyes of those two dead men; as easy to recall one as the other, Linn thought bitterly when they had completely circled the cabin and returned to the front admitting failure.

"No use, boys. Whoever it was—"

"He sure must have flew," Red glumly supplied, and adjusted the makeshift bandage over his mutilated ear. "If I hadn't been right there in sight of camp all the while I'd say it was one of them this-that-and-the-others that stole our horses. But it couldn't be. I'd take my oath

110

on that."

"Same here," Big Jack corroborated. "I wouldn't put it past none of 'em, 'specially that damn Swede. But they'd had a big fire goin' long before we got there, and they was workin' like beavers on a busted dam. They couldn't make it down and back in time."

"No, they wasn't thinkin' about a thing but gittin' that shed an' c'rell done," Red insisted.

"That pins it on someone down in this end of the Basin," Linn said. "Someone we haven't got a sight of yet. Working for Eccleson, of course—" He broke off. "I did think he was a square-shooter, but you never can tell what a man is like inside."

"Ye spoke the truth then," commented Sandy, giving Linn one of his hard piercing glances.

"Well, someone better scare up a meal of some sort. Billy, how about you and Jack? Two of us can ride over to the ranch and bring back horses for the rest, so we can get out after those the Swede got away with.

"And by the way, Sandy, did you see anything of those three, riding our horses out of the Basin?"

Sandy had not, but he explained that he had cut across from Black Coulee, saving himself five or six miles of travel, and had crossed the creek nearly a mile above where the road left the Basin. And there were too many knolls and small ridges crisscrossing the Basin to make horsemen visible from any distance. Linn had scarcely expected that Sandy would have glimpsed those three, unless he had met them where the road swung round the point of the bench that formed the south rim. And in that case Sandy would have mentioned the meeting—would undoubtedly have fought it out with them.

There was no more to be learned by talking. Linn sat down on an up-ended box beside the door and smoked,

111

hearing nothing of the talk that went on around him save the jumble of voices. He was again picturing to himself the cabin as it had looked when he pushed open the door that morning . . .

Pollo lying there in the middle of the floor, half on his side but with his face upturned, his big hat knocked sidewise; his thin straight nose, his handsome mouth with its boyishly selfish and rather sulky curve; the stubborn, cleft chin and the black hair in tumbled waves on his forehead; and most of all those long black lashes that had given his eyes their haunting languor (hiding their bold arrogance when he wished to appear at his best) . . .

The blue haze of powder-smoke, and the acrid smell of it . . . Through the smoke, the sight of Jim lying over there on the bunk dead, the snarling grin on his face, one leg in gray knitted drawers dangling over the edge . . . Linn's breath halted in his throat, held by that significant detail: Jim had been killed before he had started to get up and dress for the day.

Now that he remembered the pants thrown across the foot of the bunk (but dragging with the blanket over the edge), he wondered why he had not noticed them, thought of them, that morning. Probably because the time of Jim's death was revealed in the cold-pork hardness of his skin. Neither Sandy nor old Jerry had mentioned the fact that Jim had not started to dress—but that was because Pollo was the focal point of their thoughts, of course.

Reluctantly, almost, his thoughts swung back to the riddle of that last shot. There was a solution—there had to be. Shots didn't just fire themselves from guns which did not exist. There had been a gun in that cabin, a gun which Pollo, bursting headlong into the room, had unexpectedly faced. Someone had pulled the trigger of that gun. But who was he? Where had he gone? And furthermore, why had he returned and covered the two corpses so decorously with blankets?

His second cigarette gone cold between his lips, Linn's sharpened stare slid slowly over the four walls, the roof, the floor. Men moved before his vision as shadows obscuring briefly the place at which he was looking. Hiding places for rats he saw, but certainly nothing that could conceal a man—unless he excepted the space underneath the bunks; and from where he sat he could see to the wall under each. There was dirt, undisturbed even by a broom; old overshoes, Jim's boots, some dirty socks under Paddy's bed, three rusty traps. No evidence that a man had ever crawled under there to hide . . .

He was staring blank-eyed at the floor where Pollo had lain, seeing mentally that inert figure through smoke fog, and searching for the possible way in which the impossible could have happened, when Billy laid a hand on his shoulder and gave him a shake.

"Wake up outa that trance, Linn! Ain't you heard me telling yuh dinner's ready?" Billy's fingers clamped down affectionately before he let go. "You've been setting there looking like you was seeing ghosts."

Linn got up, opened the door and threw out his cigarette stub. "Maybe I have been," he shrugged. "Have you got any theory of how it happened?"

Billy's laugh belied the worry in his eyes. "Not a darned one. But I'll tell you what we have got, and that's some mighty good biscuits that Jack made. Drag that box up to the table, Linn, and wrap yourself around a good meal before you go tryin' to find the answer."

He bustled over to the table, pushing tin plates and

113

dishes of hot food around to make more room. "Red, you're over that way—take a look back there in that corner and see if you can find a can or something for coffee. We're a cup shy. And say, look for some sugar, will yuh, while you're huntin'? There ain't enough here to fill a honey-bee's holler tooth . . . All right, hand 'er over and I'll fill up the can. Lucky the boys had a fresh kettle of beans cooked up . . ."

There was no resisting Billy when he set himself to the task of banishing gloom from the faces around him. Even Sandy looked less dour, and old Jerry seemed on the point of becoming garrulous again. Though he felt sure the food would stick in his throat, Linn permitted himself to be badgered into pulling up to the table . . .

His next conscious thought about eating was a feeling of surprise when he found himself holding out his empty plate for Billy to spoon more beans onto it from the kettle. He lifted his tin cup to his mouth and got only a few drops of syrupy liquid with a flavor of coffee. So he had eaten and drunk.

"Y'see?" Billy grinned understandingly and reached for the coffeepot. "An empty belly never won nobody a fight; never guessed a riddle, either. Have another biscuit, Linn."

Linn had finished the beans and was eating the second half of the biscuit when the soft thudding of hoof beats approaching brought him to his feet, his hand on his holstered gun. Two long strides and he was at the door, had it open, and was staring outside.

He looked over his shoulder into the sharpened gaze of the cowboys—their eating suspended while they waited for his word. "It's Demmy Coleson," he said in a curious low tone. "I'll talk to her." And he went out, pulling the door shut against the wind. Banging it shut as if he were

114

serving notice on the boys to stay inside . . .

Demmy was sitting on her sweaty horse, her slim little body joggled with the quick heaving flanks of the winded animal. In that balmy wind her sourdough coat hung open and her sealskin cap had the storm flap turned up all around and was tilted over the right ear, letting her hair, which was the color of ripe corn, fly shining tendrils in the wind. But her face was dead white and her eyes that were blue looked almost black, and her mouth had the straight-lipped stern look which her father's had worn—was it only last night? It seemed a month ago!

"I came from the sheep camp up there," she said in a strange frozen voice. "I see you were there, all right. I must have missed you."

Slowly Linn walked toward her, chilled by that frozen calm of her voice. "You shouldn't have come," he said. "This is no place for a girl. Hell has broken loose in the Basin."

"So I discovered. Paddy kept saying 'No sheepmen— no sheepmen,' when we asked him who had shot him, so I thought I'd better come down and tell you not to start a fight with them." She paused for a quick tight breath. "I see you did, though."

"The fight," said Linn, "was started when I got there."

"Then, you boys had gone off without a thing to dress Jim's wounds or—"

"Jim's wounds didn't need dressing."

Demmy shivered, closed her eyes tightly, opened them on Linn. "I—discovered—that, too. I—came here first—"

Linn started, gave her a quick horrified glance. "You did?" He stepped closer, lifted a hand to lay it on her

115

horse's shoulder, and didn't because she twitched the reins and moved aside, out of his reach. "I wouldn't have had you in that cabin for anything in the world." The words poured out in a halfwhisper.

"No," said Demmy in that strange frozen tone. "I shouldn't think you would!"

A blow with her quirt across his face would have startled Linn less. Her tone, her look drove the words through him like needles of ice along each nerve in his body. As frozen lightning he remembered that chill flash afterwards. So swiftly it came and went that only his eyes showed he had been struck. From warm hazel they went gray-green, hard as agates in his face. But his glance did not fall before her bitter probing stare, nor could she have seen him wince and instantly brace himself. Stage training is not so easily lost. One carries on.

But his voice, if she were sensitive to its timbre, had a slightly metallic ring when he answered her, brushing aside her tacit accusation. "It wasn't a pleasant sight for a man, even. One thing you may find some comfort in knowing, Miss Coleson: Pollo died instantly; he couldn't have known what hit him."

"Oh!" she gasped, under her breath, incredulous horror widening her eyes. She caught the saddle horn with one hand as if she needed to hold herself erect, and suddenly scorn came to her assistance.

"Yes," she assented fiercely, "I suppose there is a certain satisfaction in knowing that even a cold-blooded murder has been expertly accomplished."

At his sides Linn's fingers closed tightly into his palms. "Meaning what?"

"You should know," she lashed back at him. "It had to be instant—and treacherous. If he'd seen it coming

116

Pollo's gun wouldn't be still in its holster, Mr. Moore."

Linn's pupils were dagger points probing mercilessly her suspicion of him. Then lip and eyebrow lifted together infuriatingly, lying that he was disdainfully amused with her.

"Of course," he drawled, "I'm hell on wheels when it comes to a lightning draw. You couldn't imagine me giving a man a chance, could you?"

He stepped back away from her, touched his hat, wheeled and strode to the cabin door, feeling her gaze stabbing his back as he went.

PADDY DEEPENS THE MYSTERY

OLD JERRY REFUSED POINT BLANK to stir out of the cabin that day. "I ain't no damn roadrunner," he complained. "That there walkin' four or five mile with wet feet ain't made me a doggone bit younger, Linn. I'm as stove-up as a foundered horse. You go ahead. John'll want to know the news and mebbe give yuh some diff'rent orders. Sandy's got his horse—let him go on in and bring us back something to ride. Us four'll make out here all right till mornin'." He looked around at the others with the old authority.

"Jack, you gether up all the beddin' and hang 'er out in the wind," he ordered in his mildly querulous voice that showed he was getting back to normal. "And take the tick off Jim's bunk and empty it, and fill it up with fresh hay—"

Linn nodded acquiescence. "I'll be back tonight or send the wagon with supplies and fresh horses. Sandy, you might ride back with Miss Coleson. Your horses will both need to take their time. And Jerry, if you don't mind being left afoot here I'll take Billy in with me on Pollo's horse . . ."

He remembered something all but forgotten in the shock of that encounter with Demmy. His glance went swiftly round the room. "Paddy's alive—or was—and says it wasn't the sheepmen shot him and Jim. He may be wrong; out of his head, most likely. But you might just bear that in mind, boys, and keep your weather eye peeled for whoever it was. And another thing: It was Miss Coleson who covered the boys with blankets. She came here first, missed us, and went on up the Basin."

He signed to Billy and the two went out and to the stable for the horses. Sandy and Demmy were just starting off, but Linn neither looked their way nor gave any other sign that he was conscious of the girl's presence—which impelled Billy to eye him curiously as he and Linn galloped past the other two on their tired horses.

"I don't s'pose Demmy'd want to ride a dead man's horse," Billy observed tentatively, "or she could have this one and I'd take hers on in. What'd yuh say if I asked her, Linn?"

"I'd say mind your own business," snapped Linn. But straightway he was ashamed of himself. "She wouldn't ride with me, anyway, Bill."

Bill gaped. "She wouldn't, ay? Say, you're crazy! Why, she—"

"She'll do all right with Sandy," Linn broke in acridly. "They can mill things over together and bring in a unanimous verdict. They think alike. They'll get along fine."

Billy swore an exasperated oath. "Verdict of what?"

118

And when Linn did not answer that, he rode for half a mile without speaking. "Mean to say she . . . ?"

Linn gave him a brief hard stare and turned his eyes to the front again. "I mean to say just this, Bill—" He changed his mind and closed his lips stubbornly. Then, because young McElroy was patently waiting for more, he yielded to the silent pressure. "If the sheepmen didn't do the killing, who did? It's anybody's guess from now on, and if they guess alike"—he lifted his shoulders—"I reckon that's their privilege."

A cloud settled on Billy's face. "They sure better not guess wrong," he muttered, and said no more.

They galloped steadily up over the rusty black benchland, boring into the wind that still whooped over the range.

The ranch when they rode in to the horse corral looked deserted in the dusk. But as they dismounted and pulled the saddles off their sweating horses Linn observed that the wagon which was to have hauled the boys' beds and extra provisions to the line camp now stood before the house, the team tied to a porch column near the front steps. With Billy at his heels Linn hurried up there, anxious to know the latest news about Paddy.

The two walked into a strained atmosphere of worry and indecision. The cook (they called him "Bobwhite," which may or may not have been his real name run together), dressed in his "town clothes," stood in the living room with his big hat on the back of his bald head, staring solemnly toward the open doorway of the bedroom beyond.

"I got a bed all made up in the wagon, and I aim to drive careful," he was saying when the two went in. "I don't b'lieve it'll hurt 'im none, Mis' Coleson. Paddy's tough. An' anyway—"

119

Hattie, a full-bosomed woman with a solid tread and a complexion like a healthy baby, came out of the bedroom wiping wisps of hair off her moist temples. "If you take my advice you'll leave him right where he is," she stated positively. "There's a change comin' over him right now. Whether it's for better or worse I wouldn't attempt to say, but John thinks he's comin' to his senses. You better go see what you think about him, Muriel."

Then she noticed the two standing just inside the doorway. "Well, it's about time!" she greeted them briskly. "You peel off your coat, Linn, and go in there and see what you think. Bobwhite's been pesterin' the life out of us all day long to let him haul Paddy in to Fort Benton. He's about got John talked over, and Muriel too. But *I* say that man ain't fit to be moved. He's been shot right through the stomach." (Hattie prided herself on being a perfect lady at all times, even if she did cook for the Colesons; she would never have dreamed of saying "intestines.") "Joggling would be the death of him, and I know it. So does Bobwhite, if he'd only admit it."

Bobwhite's neck stiffened. "You can't do nothin' for 'im here, and time a doctor got here he'd be dead anyway. He might jest as well die on the road as anywheres else."

Hattie gave a ladylike snort. "Hmph. All you want is a chance to get to town and *imbibe!*" she charged. "Muriel, if you listen to him—"

Linn and Billy walked past them into the bedroom, where John Coleson, gaunt and hollow-eyed, sat beside the bed. He looked up at them, shook his head significantly, and glanced down at the wounded man.

"He's quieter," he said in his deep voice that sounded

120

infinitely weary, and glanced aside as his wife came and stood at his shoulder.

She was looking at Linn. "Didn't Demeter come back with you, Linnell?"

Linn shook his head. "She's coming with Sandy, Mrs. Coleson. Bill and I rode on ahead." He saw surprise growing in her face and explained further: "Their horses were tired, and I thought we ought to get here as soon as we could. They'll be along soon."

Satisfied, she bent and looked fixedly at the face of Paddy, already shrunken and waxy-looking. "What do you think about it, John? Do you think he could stand that long ride to the hospital?"

Unexpectedly Paddy's eyes opened and glanced around the group, their faces softened and shadowed by the lighted lamp. "Don't go to no trouble haulin' me to no hospital," he said clearly. "Jim's dead and I will be; wouldn't last halfway to town. My guts is all shot to hell and that ride didn't do 'em no good, neither. Feels like a bucket uh bran mash in m'belly."

A gasp from behind them made heads turn that way. Paddy's mustache jerked up at the corners of his mouth, which signified he was trying to grin. "Stampeded the old gal that time. She's been so damn nice—nasty nice—all these years—I been wantin' to cut loose an' say somethin'—had to wait an' do it on m' deathbed—never had the nerve before."

"Don't—talk about dying, Patrick. We'll have you well and strong—" The schoolteacher voice of Demmy's mother dwindled under the sardonic look he gave her.

Then Linn took charge, moving closer to the pillow and leaning a little. "Now you've got that off your chest, Paddy, tell us this: Do you know who it was shot you

121

and Jim?"

"Hunh? Who—" Paddy's jaw hung slack. "I thought—"

"Take your time—wait a minute. Mrs. Coleson, will you get a paper and pen and write this down? It's pretty important that we get a straight, clear statement from Paddy."

A moment later, sitting on the edge of the bed, holding by the sheer power of his gaze the dying man's thoughts from wandering, he prompted again : "I'm told you kept saying, 'No sheepmen,' when they asked you about it today. Now you're feeling better and we've got to get the straight of it. Who did shoot Jim—and you?"

Paddy looked from one to the other, closed his eyes and opened them. "I shot Jim," he stated reluctantly. "Damn it, he pulled his gun on me and said he'd prove whether it was too light on the trigger or not—pointed it straight *at* me! And laid there sneerin'. I pulled my gun. Any man would. He'd be a damn fool if he didn't . . ." He licked his lips, hating to face the facts, Linn thought.

"I told him to drop that gun, and—I dunno, there was a look in his eye—he didn't drop it, and I shot him. I had to. I was afraid the damn thing would go off whether he meant it or not—and Jim's a dead shot."

"His gun was empty," Linn said. "You don't mean you killed him, that first shot?"

"Hell, no! Spoiled his aim, though—he'd-a dropped me first shot if I hadn't. Jim was a good shot . . . so I stood and shot it out. I'll meet 'im in hell tonight, I s'pose—mebby we'll start right in—where we left off. I—killed him, deader'n a mackerel. But—I couldn't shoot that—damn sarcastic grin off'n his face . . ."

Linn saw the bottle standing at John Coleson's elbow: whisky of a brand much favored on the range at that

122

time. He signaled for it; Coleson passed it to him. Mrs. Coleson, with a wide tablet on her knee, steadied it with her writing hand and handed Linn a water glass.

Linn poured a good three fingers. He didn't know what effect whisky would have on Paddy's condition, whether it would hasten death or delay it. But he knew Paddy liked his whisky straight and would go out content with the tang of it in his throat.

John Coleson moved his bony knees away from the bed, hitching back his chair a little to let Linn in there where he could slip an arm under Paddy's head, pillow and all. Paddy would have drained the glass if Linn had let him, but Linn took it away from the walrus mustache when half the whisky was down.

"More later on, Paddy. We've got to get this straight. You say you and Jim shot it out this morning— right after breakfast, wasn't it?"

Paddy left off drawing his mustache ends into his mouth and sucking them in the hope of another drop or two. "The damn' lazy hound wouldn't git up," he explained. "I bawled 'im out fer playin' off sick on me whenever we had extry work, an' he said—said—"

"Never mind." Linn's voice had an odd huskiness that sounded strange with the peremptory sharpness of his speech. "We've got that. What I want to know is, who else was there?"

Paddy gave him a glassy look. "Nobody. Who'd you think—?"

"I don't think. I don't know what to think." Linn turned to Coleson and his wife. "I didn't tell you yet, but a queer thing happened down there when we arrived." He shifted his body nervously—impatience, too, in the slight movement. "Pollo and I got off first, here. Pollo was ahead all the way and he jumped off his

123

horse in front of the camp and rushed on inside . . ." He stopped and swallowed dryly.

"I heard a shot," he said in a lower tone. "I was taking a look around outside for sign of the sheepmen—"

"No sheepmen," Paddy cut in thickly. "Jim pulled his gun on me, the damn fool—"

"No sheepmen, but I didn't know it then. I waited for Pollo or—someone to come out. No one did. I went in and—Pollo was dead. Shot through the heart."

A sharp cry came from Mrs. Coleson. Her pen dropped and rolled against Linn's muddy boot. "Apollo *dead?* That beautiful boy! So full of life and spirits—" She choked, controlled herself and caught Linn by the arm, giving it a little shake. "Who shot him? Who would do such a thing? It can't be possible! Who—"

Linn stood up, unable to endure more emotion. His laugh sounded forced and unnatural. "Echo answers *Who,* Mrs. Coleson. That happens to be the big mystery now. *Who shot Pollo?*"

He turned to the door, bumping against Billy, and stopping as if a stone wall had risen before his face. For there, just within the room, stood Demmy in her riding clothes, taking it all in.

A SHOW FOR PADDY

THEIR EYES MET AND HELD in a deep scrutinizing stare broken in an instant but seeming an unmeasured space of time to Linn. Both were pale, straight-lipped, unyielding. Both looked away, their glance going to John Coleson, who was speaking to Linn.

"Paddy'll have to sign this paper. Billy and Muriel, you can sign it as witnesses; Demmy, too. And

Bobwhite and Hattie, you come on in and sign. You both heard it—and anyway you can watch Paddy sign his name. Read it over out loud, Muriel."

"I did not," said Mrs. Coleson, in her prim schoolteacher voice which she never had laid aside except in her lightest moods, "write *verbatim*, just as Paddy told it. I stated the facts clearly, however, omitting only such irrelevant remarks as had no direct bearing on the matter."

(Just the kind of woman, Linn thought, who would hunt up the name of a goddess for her girl-child, and then mispronounce the name. A mighty fine woman, though, except for her little pretenses and small affectations.)

"Well, let's hear what you wrote," her husband testily urged her.

Whereupon Muriel Coleson cleared her throat delicately and tilted the tablet to the lamplight, read aloud the place and the date, gave another little dry cough, and read :—

I, Patrick Blake, being of sound mind and knowing that I must die, do hereby—

"He don't know no such a thing!" John Coleson interrupted her hastily. "What'd you want to go and write a thing like that for? Look at the color in his face. He's better; he's as likely to pull through as not."

"It is merely a formality meaning that Patrick is badly off and knows it, and for that reason he would not tell a lie or swear to a false statement," John's wife explained stiffly.

"Let'er ride," Paddy entreated from the pillow. "I guess I'm goin', all right. What's the rest?"

125

Mrs. Coleson began where she had left off:

. . . do hereby solemnly declare and affirm that I shot James Caplan this morning and killed him in self-defense, the said shooting being the culmination of a quarrel—

"Hold on!" Paddy held up a hand. "You got that last all wrong, Mis' Coleson. We'd been quarrelin' more or less all this mornin'. The lazy hound's been layin' down on the job all winter. It was his mornin' to start the fire—"

"This is just the formal way of telling it, Patrick," Mrs. Coleson assured him.

—of long standing. James Caplan fired six shots at me, wounding me fatally. I also emptied my gun at him, and left him lying dead in his bed.

Paddy nodded. "That's correct. Correct as hell, Mis' Coleson."

I rode in to the home ranch, and now make this statement of my own free will, for the purpose of exonerating any other person who may be otherwise accused of the killing.

Signed . . .

"All right, only I don't want to exonerate nobody but myself," Paddy observed critically while the scribe was dipping the pen and placing it in his lax fingers. "You better cut that out, Mis' Coleson, 'fore I sign it. I don't wanta git nobody into no trouble."

As if he were a child in school Muriel Coleson

126

explained, and Paddy, unabashed but satisfied, scrawled a shaky signature and lay back with a sigh of content that the job was finished.

One after the other, four names went down as witnesses—but John Coleson himself did not sign, nor did Linn.

"We might be called on to take an active part," John made vague explanation.

Now all was finished, and nothing remained for Paddy but to go out into the dark void and find Jim if he could. Linn beckoned Billy and they left the room, Linn to send Bobwhite down with the boys' bedrolls, what saddles could be found, and a string of horses that would lead.

"I'll probably overtake you on the road," he said, "I ought to wait, I suppose—"

Mrs. Coleson appeared at his elbow. "Patrick," she announced, "has taken more stimulant and he wants you to sing for him, Linnell. I—I think he is going very soon," she added in a whisper. "You mustn't deny him."

"No, I won't deny him a thing." Linn gave last directions hurriedly. "And tell Jerry if I'm not down there tonight I'll come first thing in the morning, or as soon as I can get away." Then he instinctively smoothed down his hair with his hand and went into the room.

Paddy was indeed showing the effect of the stimulant he had taken. His eyes were bright and restless and he had insisted upon having another pillow behind his head. Also he was more talkative. He flapped a welcoming hand when Linn entered, and grinned.

"If I got to go," he stated fretfully, "I sure wanna go comfortable. I want—I don' wanna go like Jim went, to the tune of six-guns poppin'. I wan' music. I never did git to hear all your singin' I wanted—I want you to

127

sing."

"Why, sure, I'll sing. All you want." At the foot of the bed Linn drew himself erect, laying his hands on the footboard as he cast hurriedly about in his mind for a suitable song.

Paddy's flapping hand stopped him just as he had filled his lungs. "Not plain singin'. Where's Demmy? What I want is—Demmy playin' the pianner and Linn singin'. I c'n die happy hearin' 'em."

Demmy's mother rose and slipped away, and presently Demmy stood, white and with red eyelids, in the room. She had changed to a blue dress, Linn noticed—blue of a shade to make her eyes look bluer than ever.

"I'll play—for you, Paddy," she said in a shaken voice, and led the way to the piano in the next room.

Neither spoke. Linn fingered a pile of music on the piano top, Demmy shuffled the leaves of a large dull green book, which he glanced at sidelong and saw was a collection called "Songs Ever New." She stood it open against the music rack while he brought a lamp from the table and set it just right, the rays falling partly on the book but mostly on Demmy's hair—not that he cared a damn for her hair, nor meant to look at the shine of it where it caught the light.

It was the opening bars of the accompaniment that snapped his thoughts to the song he was to sing. Haunting, with a majestic flow—well, did she think it was beyond him? It was "The Palms." He lifted his head, stared unseeingly out through the window beside him into the blustery night, and poured out the sweeping strains, the melody swelling like the wind out there in the dark:—

128

Blossoms and palms in varied beauty vie,
   Deck'd is the road with fragrant flowers to greet
      Him . . .
. . . Hosanna! Prais'd be the Lord!
Blessed is He who brought us salvation!

One verse of that was all Demmy seemed able to play. She was biting her lips hard before it was finished and she flipped the page and let "*O Sole Mio*" (the words in English, however) stare challengingly up at Linn. She did not look at him. For that matter, she did not need to look, since the window mirrored his reflection perfectly. And though Linn did not guess it, her eyes kept turning that way as he sang :—

How lovely is the sun in all its radiance,
How sweet the morning air, the storm departing—

He had always loved that song, always found in it a certain release. Tonight an infinite sadness, a deep loneliness beyond all words was in his voice as he sang; there, and he never knew it was there. Nor did he realize that he had forgotten to follow the printed translation, and instead had dropped into the liquid-voweled Italian through which the melody flowed as a brook flows through the grassy banks its moisture has nourished; until once more the words came, hauntingly wistful:—

Ma un sol più bello—sorride a me—

Paddy's yell, as if he were scaring a cow out of a corn patch, shattered the haunting sweetness of that last diminishing

. . . negli occhi a tel!

129

"Hey! You think I wanta die listenin' to that kinda jabberin'? I ain't no Catholic, an' this ain't no church!"

Hastily Linn went into the room and found Paddy flushed and furious. By this and by that, couldn't he have the kinda music he wanted and liked? Wasn't he the one that was doing the dying?

"When I said sing," he summed up his complaint with waggling finger, "I meant the kinda songs you sung on roundup. Coon songs. You know the kind—"

"You bet I do, Paddy. That was just to limber up my voice on. You just hold your horses."

When Linn returned to the piano Demmy was standing before it pulling sheet music out of a stack a foot high. Without a word she lifted the pile and dumped it in Linn's arms, and with swift practised hands he pulled out two pieces and set them on the piano. He called out to Paddy in a voice that made Demmy start and look at him queerly:—

"Listen to this, you highbinder, and forget your insides for a while!"

If Demmy's fingers stumbled over the keys in the opening bars, Linn paid no attention and certainly Paddy did not know the difference. Abruptly the melodious voice, that had been so caressing before, changed to a humorously plaintive tone with all the soft slurring cadences of the Southern Negro :—

Look here, Alexander, I was on-ly foolin'
When I said another coon my heart was rulin'!
   Won't yuh take me back, babe,
   And I'll always be true!

Away from Demmy and the piano, facing the open

doorway, Linn's shoulders swayed a little to the rhythm :—

. . . You can be the boss, I'll let yuh have your way—
Alexander, won't you let me stay?

Professional in every tone and look, now; forcing his mind to the task of pleasing Paddy. And from the sounds within the room, Paddy was highly pleased. Even John Coleson, bowed with mortal illness and range trouble and the loss of three men in one day, came and stood in the doorway stroking down his beard to hide the laughter behind it. Behind him, Muriel stood peering out at the singer, her face all smiling and looking a little like Demmy.

Then suddenly the dying man called out in a high, strident tone, totally unlike his natural voice: "Dammit, if they's any seein'—to be done—I wanna git in on it. It's me doin' the—dyin', ain't it? Me he's singin' fer—"

In the midst of his tearful promise to hang a washin'-sign outside his do', Linn broke off and rushed in to the bedside. "You bet it's you I'm singing for. And if we can't move the show in here, we'll move you to the show, by golly!"

From the piano stool Demmy, with her lap full of music, pretended to be searching for songs while Linn carried out two chairs and placed them alongside the wall for her parents. Not that there weren't chairs enough in the living room, but he needed them out of the way. And he knew that Demmy was watching him surreptitiously through her lashes; knew, and resented the fact . . .

But he gave no sign, nor seemed even to be aware of her presence in the room. He was busy with Paddy,

131

dragging the bed down across the doorway to where its occupant, propped on pillows and looking ghastly, could watch the performance.

"I wanna drink, first. Gotta las'—the show out. Gimme some whis-whisky—"

Curiously, it was Demmy's mother who pushed Linn toward the piano and got the bottle and glass herself, and held the scorching liquid to Paddy's lips—did it, and lost not the smallest degree of her dignity and somewhat conscious superiority. She looked, Linn thought watching her, as if she were giving the "cup of cold water to one of the least of these"—Well, perhaps it counted quite as much. Who knows what deeds are recorded as most gracious when a soul fares forth into the dark? A drink of whisky, a coon song . . .

Just within the doorway Paddy's eyes glistened in the lamplight. His walrus mustache pulled up under his nose, he laughed silently, showing his yellowed teeth when Linn sang indignantly:—

Who's dat a knockin' at de do' below?
Who's dat a shiv'rin' in de hail an' snow?
I kin heah yo' grumblin', Mister Rufus Brown!
. . . I hopes yo' freezes to death . . .

Snapping his fingers, swaying his body to the careless rhythm, Linn wondered how long death would wait; how long he could hold Paddy there enjoying this show, the vaudeville routine that had once been so hated a chore. Maybe it was worth while, after all. It was, if it could send a dying man out smiling . . . But it wasn't good enough. They liked it, Paddy most of all—but he'd like it better if Linn did it the right way; if he gave all he knew how to give . . .

132

Rufus Rastus Johnsing Brown was properly told of his misdeeds. Demmy wound up with a crashing chord or two—but it wasn't, after all, the finale that always brought roars of applause. Paddy wasn't getting his money's worth. It was good, but it ought to be better. Linn walked quickly over to Demmy.

"If you'll pardon me—this is special stuff." Eight more words than he had expected to volunteer to Demmy, but he had to give Paddy a good show. He did not push Demmy off the stool, he merely rolled the piano away from her, facing the bedroom door; rolled it halfway down the room, turned it just so, got the stool which Demmy had vacated as if it were hot, placed it with a flourish, whirled it down lower and pulled up his sleeves, his coat flung toward the brocaded plush sofa.

"Name it and you can have it!" he cried. Not Linn—at least, not the somewhat shy Linn they knew; not Linn, but "Montana Cowboy," all set to do his stuff.

Paddy responded with a cracked, whispery whoop. "By gosh—I wanna hear yuh—yodel. Boys said yuh c'n—yodel. Go on—yodel!" It was rather horrible, the way he gurgled the word.

"Yodel? You betcha." Linn gave another hitch to his shirt sleeves, thrust his brown forelock back with quick impatient fingers; dropped them on the keys, where they began to tiptoe an intricate dance up and down, like elves holding a carnival on slim black stepping-stones . . .

"Listen, my children and you shall hear how cowboys yodel in the spring of the year :—

"Way down in Cuba where the skies are clear—*whoo-oo!*"

It was the Cubanola Glide he sang, with variations of

133

his own invention—some of them improvised for
Paddy's especial enjoyment.

Glide, glide, keep on a glidin'—*Oh-lally-oo-ooo-oo*—
Slide, slide, keep on a slidin'—*Oh-oo lally-ooo-oo!*
Throw your arm around me, ain't you glad you found me,
Tease—squeeze—lovin' and wooin' . . .

Never before had he sung with Death standing by.
Never had he sung with more abandon. Billy and Sandy
came in, and stood transfixed beside the door. Vamping
intricately, impishly between verses, Linn beckoned
with a tilt of his head and the two came over, walking
on their toes.

"Go and stay with him, boys. Let me know when—"
Those mad, romping fingers never slowed nor faltered.
"I think it's about—over."

But Paddy was by no means gone on his dark journey
yet. Slumped against the pillows, he lifted his heavy lids
and waggled a hand graciously as the boys came and
stood beside the bed. " 'S great—stuff," he muttered.
"Best I—ever heard in—m'life."

"An' how are ye?" Sandy inquired.

"Dunno—don' care. Shore—gittin' a great—send-
off." And he tried to beat time; couldn't, because his
hand was too lax and heavy. "Bet Jim—never—heard
such—"

Over his head, Billy's eyes met Linn's. The message
passed unseen. Imperceptibly the tempo of the music
changed, softened, slid into another key and a sweet and
haunting melody, Linn's muted tones fluting a golden
thread of song :

There's an echo—*yoo-lally-ee-ooo*

134

In the valley—*yoo-lally—ee-ooo* . . .

More slowly, more softly, Linn's gaze upon Paddy, the two cowboys motionless . . .

Can't you hear it—*yoo-lally-ee-ooo* . . .
In the twilight—*yoo-lally-ee-ooo—oooo* . . .

Billy looked up, a finger lifted. Slowly, so very carefully, like a mother tiptoeing away from a cradle and humming under her breath as she goes, the flute tones retarded, faded into silence.

Gentle as a woman, Billy leaned, took the white knitted bedspread in his two hands, drew it up carefully, smoothing the wrinkles . . .

Linn stood up, steadying himself with a hand braced against the piano top. All at once his face was white and had the drawn look of exhaustion. He had to get away; get off by himself where he could think—where he could face the monstrous thing before him. Like a man distraught he reeled to the door and went out, slamming it behind him, shutting out the whoop of the chinook wind roaring around the corner of the house. As the door banged shut he thought he heard his name called—thought the voice was Demmy's; cursed himself for being that simple, and went staggering down to the deserted bunkhouse.

When Billy entered, ten minutes later, carrying Linn's hat and coat, Linn was lying face down on his bunk, his head pillowed on his folded arms.

135

WHO COULD BELIEVE?

"LINN! YUH IN HERE?" Billy waited in the dark, then moved over to the table and struck a match, holding it to the lampwick. Light showed him that long figure lying there slack, utter despondency revealed in the posture. He looked at it long, his face deeply worried. Sitting back against the table he pulled out his makings and made himself a smoke, preoccupied deliberation in every movement of his fingers, as if they were being left to accomplish the job automatically, without direction of the mind.

Right hand cupping the other elbow, he smoked and stared broodingly at Linn's back and legs still incased in the worn leather chaps, his spur-shanks slipped up so the rowels tilted up over the counter of his boots—at his broad flat shoulders moving a little now and then restlessly, proving he was not just lying there asleep.

Twice Billy relighted that cigarette after it had been permitted to go out; then, as if impelled to take action, he went straight over to the bunk, sat down on the widest space along the edge, and clamped a hand down on the nearest shoulder.

"Whassa molla you?" he growled, hiding his concern under facetiousness. "I s'pose that wasn't any too damn easy puttin' on a show like that. But you sure done it up brown, Linn. I've paid good money to hear worse . . ."

When he got no response from that he tried again. "It ain't Paddy, is it? He was all right, a' course, but he never was any p'ticular friend of yours—and you sure made him happy as two larks. I never seen him enjoy anything more'n he did that yodelin' of yours . . ."

Another wait, and his pleasing voice grew impatient. "Say, what the hell is eating on you, anyway? Old John wants you to come back up to the house. He wants to have a talk with you—about things."

Linn abruptly sat up. "About who shot Pollo, I suppose!"

"Hunh?" Billy started and looked at him queerly. "No, he didn't say a word about that . . ." His voice trailed off as if his thoughts had turned into another channel. "That's right," he said slowly. "Jim and Paddy shootin' it out between themselves thataway—that does kinda—"

"Kind of looks as if I'm the guilty party," Linn finished for him. "Go ahead and say it, why don't you?"

Billy flushed. "I'm capable of sayin' anything I happen to think," he retorted, half in anger. "You don't have to hand me the words, old socks. If I thought that, I'd say so."

Mechanically Linn proceeded to build a smoke. "Well, why don't you think so? It does look as if I had shot Pollo. If I didn't know I hadn't, I'd think so myself. So don't mind me, Bill. Help yourself to all the suspicion you want—while it's making the rounds."

"Say," snorted Billy, "you act like that's what you *want* folks to think! You tell me you done it, and maybe I'll kinda halfway believe it. Didja?"

Linn looked at him. "No, Bill, I didn't. That's what has got me down. I—" he hesitated. "I'd half made up my mind that by some means or other Jim's gun went off—but you heard Paddy say they both emptied their guns at each other, so . . ." He spread his hands in defeat. "The only other possibility that I can see is that I did it myself. And unless I'm crazy and don't know what I'm doing or seeing, Pollo was dead when I went

137

into the cabin. But how? In God's name, *how?*" Elbows on knees, he dropped his head between his two hands, his fingers buried in his heavy brown hair that, do what he would with comb and water, always lay in loose waves the moment it began to dry.

Young McElroy grabbed a handful now and shook Linn's head with affectionate exasperation. "Come out of it! Let other folks worry about how Pollo got shot. Even if you knew, that wouldn't bring him back to life, would it? And you've got to figure out how we're going to keep Eccleson from hornin' in on the Basin. Don't ever think you've got him stopped, Linn. There's a man that's got a mule beat for stubbornness. I betcha anything he'll be right back for more."

"Let old Jerry—"

Billy snorted. "Hunh. Old Jerry was so tickled to pass the buck to you today, you never will get him back roddin' the outfit. If you don't know it, I do—John's depending on you to see him through with this deal. Uh course," he added slyly, "if you want to let him down, that's your business. Right now when he's lost three men in one day, and sheep's crowdin' in on him, is a good time to lay down your hand—if you've got some old grudge you're tryin' to work off on a sick man."

"You talk like a damn fool," Linn charged, not looking up.

Billy pulled in a grin. "Well, maybeso. I'm only goin' by the looks of things: you setting here on your haunches holdin' your head because a man got shot kinda mysterious and you can't figure it out. If this is the time you pick for guessin' riddles, all right. I'll go on back and see if I can help John. I'll tell him you've sung yourself out and would like to hold your jaws awhile . . ." And he turned away, dragging his feet

138

noisily over the rough board floor.

Men have been lashed through blizzards to save them from death by freezing; so Billy's rough sarcasm whipped Linn's pride awake, pulling him out of the dangerous lethargy that had fogged his mind like a drug.

Billy had not taken the third step when Linn had him by the shoulder. "You win. Thanks. I'd no business to cave in like that. But I—I never went up against the job of yodeling a man out of his body before. It was—pretty awful, Bill—it got me."

"Sure, it got you. It'd get anybody. It was pretty damn white of you, if yuh ask me. I s'pose—yuh think we better take him outa there, Linn? Kinda tough on the women folks, havin' to sleep with a corpse in the house—"

For answer Linn jerked open the door, cursing himself for his weakness. And Billy, following him out, seemed satisfied that the cure was complete. At any rate he said no more, offered no further suggestions. That, his manner said, was up to Linn and John Coleson.

Sandy was alone with the boss in the living room when they went in. Whatever they had been saying, their conversation ceased abruptly when the two entered. The bedroom door was closed and a draught blew out through the crack under the door, indicating that a window in the bedroom had been opened. The piano was back in its usual place, closed and with the stool pushed back as far as it would go under the hidden keyboard. But on the music rack *O Sole Mio* stared enigmatically at Linn, pricking his sore nerves like the jab of a needle in his arm.

Because he was certain that was Demmy's doing, deliberately wanting to hurt him, he turned away and fixed his eyes and his attention upon his boss. Coleson,

139

he thought, looked almost as ghastly as Paddy had done before the liquor took hold of him. The old man sat in a morris rocker, his bony hands gripping the arms as if he were bracing himself against some deadly pain, but whether it was mental or physical Linn could not guess.

"Sandy tells me you burned out the sheep camp, and let them set you afoot while you was doing it," he began abruptly. "I'd like to hear the particulars. But call Demmy first, will you? She'll want to hear it too, I s'pose—seeing she's trying to learn the business."

Linn hesitated, then went into the kitchen and delivered the message to Hattie, thus evading a direct encounter for a little longer—hating himself, too, for dreading to face Demmy. What difference did it make, anyway? She only thought what they'd all be thinking before long, even if they didn't now. He might as well get used to it.

Coleson waited in complete silence until the girl came in and sat down beside him, laying her hand over one of his where it rested on the chair arm; holding it there in a firm clasp. They looked, Linn thought, rather at bay; as if they were taking their stand together against rather long odds; they looked, too, as if they were prepared to stand alone if necessary . . . Not begging for loyalty, scarcely even expecting it— and the fact that Paddy and Jim had placed their own petty quarrel ahead of the Triangle J's welfare made their apparent withdrawal seem justified. If it developed that Pollo and Linn had likewise attended first to their private grudge . . . Linn set his teeth and waited, his eyes on the father and carefully avoiding the girl.

Coleson cleared his throat. "Before we go into the sheep question," he said in his harsh tired voice, "I want all you three can tell me about them killings. I'll have to

140

make a report to the sheriff, I s'pose. He won't take any action unless I tell him he's wanted . . . We're kinda outa the way, off up here, and so fur we've had no dealin's with the law . . .

"So I'll send in Paddy's statement, and that'll account for them two all right. But he don't make no mention of Paul Ganzer gettin' killed, so I've got to report it accordin' to facts, if I can get hold of 'em." His keen old eyes moved from face to face, turning at last to the girl beside him.

"Demmy, you go git that tablet and pen your mother had—and write down what the boys report. Then I'll make up my mind what to tell Joe Ellis. He's the sheriff," he added, looking at Linn. "Now," he went on when Demmy had settled herself—suddenly looking like a stenographer, Linn saw with some astonishment—"now, I'm going to ask questions if I feel like it. But you start in and state the facts as you know'em. Who got there first?" (He must have known, Linn thought. He was merely setting aside everything except this present report.)

Linn spoke: "Pollo—Paul Ganzer—reached the cabin before I did. A half-minute, I should say. He started ahead of me and kept the lead all the way. I was just riding down into the hollow when he jumped off and ran in the door, slamming it shut behind him. I was close enough to hear it bang shut."

Coleson was stroking his beard, concentrating on the reply. His head, dropped forward a little, let a rim of muddy white show under the blue irises as he gazed at Linn. "You go right on in?"

"No, I swung over toward the corral and stable, looking for tracks. I spent possibly another half-minute scouting around. Then I heard a shot fired inside the

141

cabin—"

"You'd swear to that?"

"Yes." Linn clipped the word. "I'd swear to that. You may consider that I'm speaking under oath now, Mr. Coleson. I heard a shot fired inside the cabin. I jumped my horse around to where I had a clear view of the door and front window, slid off, and stood behind him with my gun across the saddle. I expected, of course, that someone would show. If it were one of the sheepmen, I'd have a bead on him."

Unconsciously Coleson nodded approval to that—as if he would have done just that himself. "How long did you wait there?"

"I don't know. I can time myself riding down that hollow, and also riding around in the edge of the brush looking for tracks. I know the ground I covered. But standing there watching the cabin is a different proposition. I think I stood there at least a minute or two. No longer, I'm sure. Sandy and Jerry were coming along behind, and they hadn't shown up when I left my horse and went inside." Linn's teeth clicked together. It was horrible, having to go all over it again tonight. He wondered fleetingly how Demmy was going to stand it.

Coleson drew himself up in his chair, took a fresh grip on the chair arms, and sighed heavily as if he too were finding this more of an ordeal than he had anticipated. "Now, tell exactly what you found inside; everything you saw."

Linn's eyes flashed a glance at Demmy's hands on the tablet. She was taking shorthand, he noticed. Her knuckles were white and her pencil was digging in pretty hard, but her hands were steady . . .

"I ducked in and stood with my back against the wall and my gun up. I had to wait a second or two for my

142

eyes to accustom themselves to the dimmer light. I was facing the bunks and I saw Jim Caplan lying half on his side with his gun held tightly in his hand, pointing it in my direction. I slid a little to one side, over toward the table—just instinctively to get out of line.

"But Jim was dead." (After all, Demmy had been in that cabin and had seen what he saw. She knew what was coming; she was braced to listen.) "Pollo was lying on the floor in front of the bunk, dead—shot through the heart, I believe; or so close to it death must have come instantly."

Coleson's eyes bored into Linn's face. "And how," he asked, "do you account for the killing?"

Linn's eyebrows drew together. "I don't account for it. I can't. The room was full of gunsmoke . . ."

While he talked, setting that amazing scene vividly before them, Demmy's pencil went on and on, making little hooks and lines looped at the end like the twist in a pig's tail. From the corner of his eye Linn watched her fingers recording every word he spoke—recording accurately, he knew, since he had a rusty knowledge of shorthand . . .

" . . . I went out and waited outside the door till Jerry and Sandy rode up. They went in and saw what I saw, except that the smoke had thinned a little by then. There were no tracks outside except what we made ourselves. Sandy can tell you that."

There, she had it down; all he could tell, all he knew. Hot irons could not have dragged the story out of him for her satisfaction, and yet she had it all. It sounded crazy—not even a smart lie, after what Paddy had told them. She didn't believe it. No one would.

DEMMY HUNTS EVIDENCE

SANDY TOLD HIS STORY with meticulous exactness, haggling with himself over the smallest details: the exact position of both bodies, the rigidity of the corpse on the bunk. He surprised Linn, startled him even, with one angle of reasoning.

"It could be that Linn shot Pollo himself," he said, "and made haste to clean his gun barrel before we came. It would take quick work and quick thinking, and to my mind he's well capable of both. But I looked for gun oil in the cabin, and found none of the kind we all used last night, which has a peculiar smell. There is one can on a shelf, a swab not lately used beside it, but it's that cheap stuff they sell at Overman's, and the stink of it there's no mistaking. I couldna smell it on Linn's gun, which had a verra faint smell of the oil he used last night."

"Then you can swear his gun was not fired in the cabin?"

But Sandy shook his head with true Scottish obstinacy. "I couldna swear that it was not, John. There could have been a bottle of the gun oil we have here—it surprised me that there was not. Linn could have swabbed out his gun and thrown the bottle in the bushes. I do not say he did that, but I canna swear that he did not. He was standing outside with his gun hanging loose in his hand when we rode up."

John Coleson asked a question then: "Did you look for the bottle in the bushes?"

"I did not. But I looked in the stove and in other places for the swab, and found no sign of it. I didna look for the bottle outside."

Coleson pulled his beard thoughtfully. "Unless he did clean his gun, then, he didn't shoot Paul Ganzer. That's the size of it, ay?"

Sandy stuck to his caution. "Unless he cleaned his gun immediately after he shot Pollo, he did not shoot him—with his own gun." He moved restlessly in his chair. "The man lay dead with a bullet hole through him, front to back. Ye know well, John, bullets do not fly with wings of their own. And there was gun smoke in the cabin when we went in."

For the first time since the questioning began Demmy looked up, a straight keen glance searching Linn's face; meeting his eyes with a swift clash of mind against mind, as if two swords had met in combat, hard and bright and questing for vulnerable points left unguarded. Meeting, holding together and falling apart with nothing gained for either—nor lost, since that sweet new comradeship had crashed between them at the cabin.

Then her father spoke to her and she turned her eyes away, looking down as she flipped leaves, reading back through Sandy's longwinded statement. No, she said finally, Sandy had said nothing of how Linn's gun barrel felt when he examined the gun.

"It was cold," Sandy admitted—reluctantly, Linn thought. "But one shot wouldna heat it, John."

"In winter," John Coleson stated authoritatively, "a gun is cold. You know that. One shot would take off the chill from the barrel, I'm pretty sure."

Demmy spoke unexpectedly, her gaze still upon her notes. "I have a gun on my saddle, hanging under the shed. Get it, Billy—holster and all."

With a quick startled glance at Linn, Billy got up and went out, the lamp blaze flaring up the chimney in the wind as he opened the door. Coleson had no more than filled his pipe when the door opened again. Without a word, Billy handed the girl her holstered gun. His face was a study in repressed indignation.

Demmy did not look at him, but at Sandy. She swung the gun over to him by the holster belt. "Take it and feel the barrel, will you?" Her voice sounded as if she were rather consciously holding it steady. "It has been outside, and the weather is about the same as this morning."

Sandy nodded, apparently seeing nothing strange in the test. He withdrew her gun, a silver-mounted .45, and ran his fingers slowly over the barrel, frowning in deep concentration.

"As cold as that?"

"I think—I couldna swear to it—but the feel is about the same," he replied cautiously.

"Well, take it out on the porch and fire one shot. In about two minutes—or three?—feel it again."

Linn's lip curled. She was rubbing it in with a vengeance. Even Billy McElroy was glaring at her now, and her father's impatience was so apparent that she answered his unspoken reproach as Sandy hesitated, one hand on the doorknob.

"As far as possible we should test for evidence, Dad. Don't you see? I'm sure if I were involved I should insist on every possible test to prove my story." She was so careful not to appeal to Linn, not to look at him, that she rather emphasized her avoidance. Even her father noticed that, and looked at Linn curiously.

They heard the shot, and they waited. "The cabin was cold as a barn," said Demmy to no one in particular. "He'll stay on the porch . . ."

They waited while the clock tick-tocked the seconds and the minutes. Demmy, it appeared, was measuring

146

the time on her watch, her head bent. Hattie opened the dining room door, said, "Supper's ready!" and stood there staring at those silent four until Demmy squelched her with a glance which sent her back where she came from; the door slammed behind her.

They waited. A mental reaction held Linn detached, even slightly amused at this hairsplitting. Let her go ahead, try all she could to prove him a liar . . .

"It's colder tonight than it was this morning," he heard himself saying. "Better call him in, Miss Coleson. I'm willing to let it go at a minute and a half, allowing for the difference in temperature."

"Thank you. I had thought of that," she said evenly, and went and opened the door.

Sandy came in, went through the useless performance of feeling the gun barrel. Demmy reached over and laid her own fingers upon it.

"Cold," she said, and made notes.

Of a sudden John Coleson gave a snort of anger. "Cold or hot, this boy's word goes with me," he declared. "There ain't a thing to show he killed Ganzer. If he had, he'd of cooked up a better story than the one he told. Any fool would know that much."

"Pollo's—dead," said Demmy, her voice threatening to break. "Somebody did it. Someone who never gave him a chance; someone he never dreamed was going to shoot him—or he'd have drawn his own gun."

"Well, talkin' won't bring him to life again. I ain't going to have Joe Ellis fiddlin' around out here when it won't bring back any one of the three. Linn Moore's story stands, far as I'm concerned. There's nothing to contradict it—"

"Except Pollo—shot through the heart." Again that half-break in her voice. She pressed her lips together,

147

swallowed dryly, her face dead-white.

Her father gave her a sharp look, brought his hand down with a slap on the chair arm. "If you're going to learn how to run this outfit, Demmy," he said sternly, "you got to cut out actin' like a schoolgirl. Use your head. Think I'm going to hold up everything and let Eccleson come in and sheep me out while we go bawling around pawin' up the ground like a cow-funeral, tryin' to figure out how Ganzer got shot? That'll come to light some day, maybe. Time enough to do something about it when it does."

Life had come into his dull eyes, a new timbre into his voice. He looked at the three cowboys sitting there watching him gravely. "Pass on the word to the boys to keep their eyes open and their mouths shut. I'll write and tell Joe that three of my boys shot it out, down in the line camp, and no survivors left for him to arrest."

"But, Dad—"

"I'm runnin' this, Demmy. Mebby it'll learn you how to handle our own business accordin' to justice and common sense, and not git tangled up with the courts. That gives an outfit a bad name."

His eyes turned to Linn. "In the morning, I guess you better take Paddy's body back down there and bury the three of 'em together. Pick out a nice place, and put up headboards—give 'em as decent burial as time and circumstances will allow."

"Yes sir, I'll see to it first thing in the morning."

Coleson nodded. "You ain't through with Eccleson, not by a long chalk. Now, about them sheep—I want to know all the ins and outs of what took place. Sandy says you burned 'em out, and they stole your horses. How'd that happen?"

They talked of the sheep problem and what means

148

must now be taken to get their horses and saddles back. Linn forced himself to set all other matters to one side, to focus his thoughts on that one point. He even sat at table opposite Demmy, ate and drank and saw that she was making only a thin pretense, and held his mind and his heart rigidly aloof from her.

John Coleson was a sick man, and he was in trouble. He trusted Linnell Moore to see him through, to hold Shadow Basin against the sheep. Just when they were most needed, three men were gone. Well, he would have to do the work of those three, then; he and the others. The old man was right. This was no time to run in circles trying to pick up the trail of the truth. No time, either, to care what Demmy thought or didn't think about him. He wasn't working for Demmy, exactly. It was John Coleson who had hired him.

That night they did what must be done, made what preparations were possible. And contrary to his expectations Linn slept heavily until nearly dawn. He felt rested, able to meet whatever exigencies might arise that day, able to officiate at the burial of three men and go on to the next task. He roused the other two, rolled his bed and roped it, went down and fed the horses they would use that day, met the boys, and gave them their orders with a matter-of-fact calm.

They would hitch one of the hay-hauling teams to a wagon and take Paddy back to the Basin right after breakfast. Linn had already started a fire in the mess house and had the coffee on, and he would light out, he said, as soon as he had eaten a snack, and have everything ready when they came . . .

All planned to the smallest detail, to permit a burial with at least a measure of decorum and yet leave nearly the full day for what might befall . . . So much time for this, so much for that, and let him be in at least two places at once (approximately) ... He had himself in hand, and was conscious of the fact. He told himself he'd be a fighting machine from now on and not indulge himself in any emotion whatsoever.

So he galloped purposefully across the bench and down the hill and into the Basin, feeling very sure of himself indeed—absolutely indifferent to what Sandy or Demmy or anyone might believe. He spent some time deciding whether to repeat the Twenty-third Psalm or the Lord's Prayer, and rehearsed them both to himself, just to see which one he remembered the more accurately; found that he had forgotten parts of both, and wished he had thought to borrow a Bible.

He hummed certain tunes, mentally fitting in the words—because he meant to sing a hymn. Paddy would prefer the "Cubanola Glide," no doubt, but Paddy had nothing to say about this ceremony ... Linn was astonished to discover that he did not know all of the words of any hymn. Snatches here and there, and that wouldn't do ... He had no intention of making a fizzle of the brief ceremony he planned. Well, how about "The Palms," then? A grand sweeping rhythm . . . or "Jesus, Lover of my Soul." Maybe the boys would join in on that ...

He was deciding in favor of the old hymn, and feeling pretty sure he could get through the first verse all right, when he rode down into the hollow that held the line camp. Suddenly a hot rage blazed up within him, made him grind his teeth at his own helplessness to strike back somehow.

For there was Demmy walking slowly with her head bent and her gaze concentrated on the ground, looking for a certain flat bottle with a rather stubby neck, that

150

would smell like a certain brand of gun oil. Walking back and forth in the old weeds and bushes within throwing distance of the door . . .

GRAVES FOR THREE

THAT WINDY MORNING the ground was wholly bare. If there were a bottle of any kind flung out in the brush, Demmy should be able to find it. Cans there were, plenty of them, it being the habit of line camp cooks to open the door and send cans sailing out, to land where they would. Several times while Linn was riding toward her, holding in his horse, the girl paused to give closer inspection to some object on the ground.

As he came up she stopped and picked up a bottle, looked at it and sniffed, then tossed it aside. Her lifted eyes met Linn's sardonic gaze.

"Lemon extract," she said.

"Keep on looking," he advised as he swung down from the saddle twenty feet away, yanking his hat tighter on his head.

"I mean to," she retorted, and poked at something with her boot toe. She stooped, picked up a tin can, dropped it. She had her back to him now and she did not look around as he walked toward her heading for the door.

"I'll get the boys out here to help hunt," he volunteered dryly as he passed, and saw with bitter satisfaction the flush that stained her cheek nearest him, showing the shot had not missed.

"Yes, do!" she retorted in a tone to match his own. "But let them finish breakfast first. They're loafing this morning." And she went on with her search, moving farther away from him and scrutinizing every object on the ground as she came to it.

Linn gave a soundless snort and opened the door upon a heated argument that must have been going on for some time.

"Call it a ghost—anyway, it sure wasn't nothin' human fired that shot." This was Bobwhite, frying pancakes and stating his views defiantly, his back turned to the door as Linn stepped in.

Red's bellow covered the entrance. "Aw-w, come off! A ghost packin' a six-shooter is a new one on me! What went with the gun? That blink out, too? And yuh take notice that wasn't no vanishin' bullet; that there was a lead slug that killed him. So where'd you git off at?" He became suddenly aware of Linn and pulled his mouth down humorously at the corners. "Bobwhite here's got it all figured out that Pollo was shot by a ghost," he explained. "S'pose he thinks that the Black One, as they call it, got in his dirty work, or something."

"Hunh!" old Jerry grunted sourly. "Sure took him a long time to git around to it." He stirred his coffee morosely and drank.

Still standing with his back to them, Bobwhite tossed the frying pan expertly, flipping a large golden-brown cake. "Well, he done a good job when he did git to it, didn't he? And if it was done by a human man, you tell how he done it. I heard Paddy myself, sayin' there wasn't nobody but him and Jim around here. Then Pollo comes in and gits his. And Jerry claims Linn Moore never done it—hell, maybe you think Pollo's layin' out there in the shed playin' off! Think he just imagines he's dead, I s'pose! If it wasn't Linn, it sure musta been a ghost."

He turned and saw Linn and had the grace to look

embarrassed. But he was too old a range hand not to have nerve. "Speak of the devil—he couldn't come, this early in the mornin', so you might tell us your theery, Linn. If it so happens yuh got one." And he slid the pancake deftly onto the rapidly diminishing pile on a plate.

Linn's teeth came together. Pollo was going to be much more unpleasant dead than he had been alive, more harassing and more formidable an enemy. It was as if his bold mocking stare met Linn whichever way he turned.

"I only wish I did have, Bobwhite," he said, trying to keep his voice natural. "I admit it's too deep for me. Looks as if the Black One and I will have to toss up to see which one shoulders the blame."

Bobwhite's jaw sagged. " 'T'ain't nothin' to josh about," he protested weakly. "Them old Injuns never give this Basin the go-by for nothin', you can bank on that." He dribbled batter on the stove when he poured another cake into the pan, he was so perturbed. "I never did have no use for that damn Shadder pointin' his finger down this way like he does!" he blurted nervously. "Maybe he didn't do it, but—"

"Why not try Sandy's theory?" Linn was pouring himself a cup of coffee, his gloves tucked into a side pocket. His hands were steady as a rock. He wanted to fight something, have someone accuse him openly so that he could contend against something tangible.

"What one's that?" asked Red, though he must have known—or at least guessed.

Linn gave a reckless laugh, looking at Red across the steaming cup. "Oh, Sandy guesses maybe I shot Pollo myself."

"All damn poppycock!" snorted old Jerry. "He knows
153

damn well your gun——"

"Sandy has that all figured out, now." Linn took a tentative sip, found the strong brew scalding hot and blew a tiny ripple below the steam. "He thinks I could have fired the shot, hustled around and found some gun oil of that stinking kind at the ranch, found a rag, wiped out my gun, and slipped in a full cartridge—and swallowed the empty shell, I suppose—and went out and stood in the wind to make sure my gun barrel wouldn't show any warmth to the touch." While they stared he took a swallow of coffee, his eyes meeting their glances as he looked from face to face.

"It would have been possible, all right. We tried out a gun at the house last night. As a theory it beats your ghost, hands down, Bobwhite. Sandy says I'm smart. He even thinks I'd be smart enough to chew the rag and throw the bottle of oil out in the brush. Demmy Coleson's out there now looking for it. I told her I'd send some of you boys out to help her hunt."

With a surprised look old Jerry half rose from his place and looked out through the high window. "Demmy knows that ain't so. She said she'd look for tracks while we et." He sat down again looking worried. "She was just foolin' yuh, Linn. She don't think——"

Linn's shoulders lifted. "I don't know why not," he intercepted Jerry's disclaimer. "I might, myself, if I didn't happen to know better. And being smart—according to Sandy—I might go even farther than they do. I might say it was planned in advance (though I admit I'd have to be a mindreader and a prophet to know it would work out this way). I might have packed a bottle of that particular brand of gun oil and a rag with me, so I could wipe out my gun."

Again he looked round the group. "Any of you

fellows like to smell my pockets?"

Red got coffee down his windpipe and could not speak his mind. Slow, silent Jack Smithers shook his head and grinned a sickly refusal. Jerry gave his habitual grunt.

Bobwhite gave him a shrewd glance. "Well, you got inside infermation on that. What *do* yuh think? No good smellin' around now fer oil," he opined. "If you was sharp enough for all that, you're sharp enough to git rid of the smell."

Red recovered breath then and swore. "You wouldn't shoot a man down without givin' him a chance to go for his gun, would yuh?"

Their eyes met in a straight hard stare. It was Red's that slid away embarrassed. "'Course, I don't think for a minute you would."

"No, I wouldn't. And with two men already shot, and a fight on our hands, I'd hardly have chosen just this time to kill one of the hardest fighters in the bunch. You saw yourselves that Pollo hadn't made any threatening move toward me or anyone else. I'd have had to do it in cold blood—and take a damn poor time to do it."

He began to draw on his gloves as the men finished the meal. "And this is about as poor a time to try and guess how it happened," he added crisply. "If you fellows are through, we'd better get out and start digging. Mr. Coleson wants the boys buried here somewhere, this morning, since there's no time nor opportunity for the conventional ceremonies."

He looked at Jerry, who was getting up stiffly. "If you feel like riding, you could take my horse and come show me where to have the graves dug. Jack and Red, better rustle all the tools you can find. The boys are bringing Paddy's body, I suppose Miss Coleson told

155

you. They're bringing extra horses, so we can get out and hunt ours as soon as we're through here."

The group swung into action, getting hats and gloves, buckling on guns and buttoning coats against the wind that still blew hard from the southwest. What words they spoke were of small duties connected with the somber task before them : there would be a pick and shovel down by the water hole in the creek; another shovel at the stable; maybe a pick out by the hay-corral. Already the necessity of giving Pollo's handsome body to the earth had pushed into the background of their minds the manner of his death. The business of living must go on regardless.

With old Jerry at his heels Linn went out and led up his horse, that the old man might ride even the short distance they must go to find a burying place. Demmy was already on her horse, waiting; and if she was disappointed to see old Jerry climbing into Linn's saddle she gave no sign as she reined over that way.

"I'll show you where I think is the best place for—for the graves," she said, speaking to Jerry as she came up. "Just back there at the head of the hollow, where it flattens out this side of the cottonwoods."

Though she did not glance at him, Linn felt that her directions were really meant for himself, and her next words proved he was right.

"We may as well do a little scouting around, Jerry, don't you think? We'll have an hour or more to wait, I suppose."

"All of that," Linn told her briefly, and walked on toward the stable, falling into step beside Red. He did not glance their way when the two rode off together, yet when the turn of the trail brought them directly before his eyes he could not turn his eyes away so long as they were in sight. He was wishing profoundly that they would extend their ride until this was over. Primitive burial such as this must be was not going to be easy for a girl like Demmy Coleson to watch, especially when her Greek-god admirer was to be laid away uncoffined, a gray blanket his only shroud.

Red found and shouldered a pick, Linn picked up a shovel at the stable and led the way to the tiny flat. The marks of shod hoofs in the soft soil gave silent proof of Demmy's inspection. Even the graves—three of them—had been staked off with dead stubs of cottonwood limbs, and the imprint of her riding boots showed here and there . . .

Where she had stood at the head of the right-hand grave Linn set his teeth and drove in the shovel point, cutting one footprint through at the instep. Pollo's grave. As if she had left the name there he knew that this was the one, a double space between it and the other two; set apart, just as his death stood alone, wrapped in mystery. Linn put a booted foot on the shovel's shoulder, pressed the blade deep. With the first clod of earth he tossed aside he threw away the thought that Demmy had been thinking of him when she stood there; thinking of him and wondering how she could contrive to have him dig that grave; him and none other. She had wanted it as a retribution for Linn Moore. Or so he firmly believed.

Very well, then. This grave and none other he would dig.

TROUBLE'S NOT BURIED

IF DEMMY ACTUALLY HAD some such penance in mind for Linn, her manner gave no hint of it when she rode back into the hollow leading two horses behind her— saddled horses, rolled overcoats tied behind the cantles. A little distance behind her came Jerry with three more.

Standing waist-deep in the hole he had dug, Linn lifted a shovelful of sandy soil, tossed it on the reddish pile beside him, and climbed out, unaccustomed muscles protesting against the violent exercise he had given them. So long were the steps he took that he was at the corral in time to take the lead-ropes from Demmy and tie the horses to the fence. One was his own tall brown. He wondered if she realized that, when she started out with it; certainly she must now, unless she refused to notice how the horse teased for petting . . .

"Say Linn, them skyoodlers hazed these horses clean back into the Basin!" old Jerry was telling him with, a grim kind of satisfaction. "We was over across the creek lookin' to see where them sheep is now, and we seen three riders bringin' our horses back. Sure is a good thing they did—fer if Eccleson had of kept 'em till we went after 'em, John sure as h-henry would of went to the ground with him. Had 'em across a bar'l then for horse-stealin'. We could of made 'em sweat for that, all right."

Demmy lifted her head impatiently. "Oh, save all that for bunkhouse talk, Jerry." Her eyes flashed to Linn's face. "The sheep are headed this way, but they're spread out feeding, or trying to. And the men who brought our horses went right on up the Basin. I'm almost certain a wagon has gone in, too, but the road is so cut up now I couldn't be sure. We had to get the horses here first of all—"

"Yeah, the sons uh guns turned 'em loose, quick as they seen us comin'," Jerry cut in there. "Looked to me like they poured the quirt to 'em, too, to git 'em scattered and runnin'. We been all this time ketchin' 'em, or we'd of been back quicker. They wouldn't drive—them gosh darn Swedes had 'em plumb wild. Hung themselves up in the brush, or we never would of caught 'em without help."

Again Demmy waited with impatience until he had finished. "I'm going back to make certain of that wagon track. As soon as you boys are through here—"

Linn raised unreadable eyes to her. "Oh. Aren't you going to stay for the funeral?"

He saw her wince, saw her catch her breath. The skin around her nostrils turned dead white. But she could not evade his searching eyes, and her voice when she spoke was firm and without emotion.

"I think you are qualified to officiate, Mr. Moore. There's nothing I can do here to help—anyone. I'll go and see if they had the nerve to go back up the Basin." She edged her horse half around, with an expert touch on the reins so that her back was squarely toward certain mournful activities up near the cabin where the wagon holding Paddy's still form was being drawn up alongside the shed door.

"Don't go too close to that camp," Linn admonished in a tone he had not meant to use. "If they're back, they've come loaded for bear. We don't want another—" He caught back the words unspoken.

"I know one thing," Jerry broke in gruffly. "You ain't goin' near that camp. What you're goin' to do is hit the

159

trail for home. You'd no business to come in the first place. You go on, Demmy. 'Tain't no place fer womenfolks."

"Oh, isn't it!" She gave them both an indignant look and spurred her horse straight out through the brush, cutting across the hollow to the trail. (Once before she had wheeled in just that mood and dashed off like that at breakneck pace through brush and rocks, riding with the careless grace of a boy. That day Pollo had spurred after her. This morning he was close and gave no heed to her flight.)

"That darn kid don't know the meanin' of fear," old Jerry grudgingly declared as they watched her go. "One thing—I sure put a bug in her ear, about that shootin', Linn. That damn' Scotchman had been fillin' her head . . . ."

"That makes no difference now," Linn cut him short. "We can do all there is to do here, Jerry. I'd cut in ahead and see that she doesn't get up there at that camp, if I were you. Hold her back from there if you have to tie her," he gritted. "That damn Swede . . ."

"Yeah, I'd have a swell chance of tying her!" Jerry snorted. "Recollect, I helped raise that kid. She takes a notion to do a thing, all hell couldn't stop 'er!"

"She'd think all hell was trying to," snapped Linn, "if I didn't have my orders to bury these boys. Of course, I'm not giving you orders, Jerry—"

"Oh, I'll go," Jerry grumbled, and stuck a reluctant foot in the stirrup of his own saddle. "I kinda wanted to be here and—kinda give them boys so-long," he made wistful confession. "Seems kinda scaley to put anything else ahead of their funeral. Me and Paddy come up the trail together on the first drive the Triangle J ever made up outa the Panhandle. He sure wouldn't ride off and leave me—"

160

Lip caught between his teeth, Linn reached out and put a hand on Jerry's knee in its old batwing chap-leg. "That's different," he said softly. "You stay and see Paddy through with it. I didn't know—"

He glanced toward the trail where it lipped over the hollow's brim. "I guess there's no such rush, anyway. Time she rides down to the mouth of the Basin and picks up that wagon track and follows it, we'll be through here and we can cut straight across and get up there ahead of her, all right."

The wagon with its added burdens was moving out away from the shed, clucking over the rocks toward the cottonwoods. Linn swung into the saddle and the two reined in behind the wagon, riding at a walk. Billy, bowlegging hurriedly to the corral, got his own horse and spurred to join them, and the little procession climbed the gentle slope, Sandy trying to avoid the rough spots.

One prayer was made to serve for the three shrouded figures resting in those shallow graves: the Lord's Prayer, reverently intoned by Linn standing impartially as near the upper center of the row as he could, the others mumbling such phrases as they could recall; Jerry loyally close to Paddy's head, the others less consciously choosing their places. Inadvertently Linn condensed the prayer, forgetting the line about forgiving our trespasses, until it was too late—though he atoned for that by adding an especial plea for the welfare of the unshriven souls of the three.

The song, too, was chosen impulsively at the last minute. With Demmy haunting his worried mind, he could not think of the ones he had tentatively rehearsed that morning, but instead found himself singing:—

We shall meet beyond the river
  Where the surges cease to ro-oll—
Where in all the bright forever
  Sorrow ne'er shall press the soul.

And the rough voices of the others, somewhat off-key, joined self-consciously in the chorus:—

We shall meet—we shall meet—
We shall meet be-yond the—riv-err—

Far upwind, faint but unmistakable, three shots barked a staccato warning (or it could have been a signal for help), and the hymn halted abruptly at that discordant river. Linn slapped his hat on his wind-rumpled hair, yanked the brim down over his forehead as he ran for his horse.

"Throw in some dirt, boys, before you leave—you can finish the job afterwards!" And he was gone, clods from his horse's feet flung back to the suddenly busy group. One clod fell on Pollo's blanket-swathed form, was followed by others, two shovels working like mad . . .

Old Jerry, swearing incoherent oaths, made haste to his horse, throwing himself into the saddle as if he were a young hell-for-leather cowboy like the rest—not an old ranny all stove-up from hiking four swearing miles in his high-heeled boots. Down the trail the battering thud of Linn's horse running on soft ground receded, was lost.

Billy McElroy, plying his shovel furiously, tossed it to Jack, who was scraping dirt over the edge with the flat side of a pick. Jack grabbed the shovel, set it deep in the red pile, one slanted glance following Billy as he tore out after the others. Then Sandy was through and gone, and Jack—Bobwhite climbing heavily up over the wagon wheel to the seat, because he was no good on horseback and he couldn't see to shoot straight. Somebody had to stay and tend camp . . .

And the dead, if they knew, must have found their hell in being unable to rise up and ride with the rest.

MORE TROUBLE AHEAD

BEYOND A WIDE GRAVELLY WASH with straightcut banks Demmy reined her horse, wheeling it to face Linn. "Those three shots? Yes, of course I fired them." Across the space that separated them her voice sounded cold as new ice.

"Well, what was the trouble?"

"Nothing—at least, no attempt is being made on my life, if that's what brought you on the run," she told him. "I merely signaled, so you wouldn't all go chasing off up the Basin by the short cut. Are the boys coming?"

"They are." Linn's face was stern. "What's on your mind?"

"If you'll ride over here, I'll show you. There's a band of sheep in this Basin, and they must have come in during the night—unless," she added sarcastically, "you failed to drive them all out."

Frowning, Linn put his horse across to where she waited. Demmy was pointing to the little cloven prints of many sheep. The tracks were fresh, certainly had been made since the chinook had started. He looked, then beckoned to Jerry, who was galloping to join them.

"How many bands has Eccleson got, Jerry? I thought you said the sheep were out on the flat, grazing along this way."

163

"They was," grunted Jerry, scanning the tracks with unbelieving eyes. " 'Course, we only rode to where we could look across and see 'em over there, and they was scattered out over them little ridges runnin' down to the crick. But it sure looked to me like them two bands we throwed together day b'fore yesterday." He stared again at the telltale sign. "I d'no how many bands he's runnin' this winter," he said. "It looks to me like he's figuring on movin' right in bag an' baggage!"

"I thought I'd cut across here into that trail they've made up the Basin," Demmy explained, looking at old Jerry. "I thought it would save time and travel, and naturally if the wagon tracks I'm sure I saw were going back up to that camp, I could pick them up along the meadow where it's soft. So when I saw this sheep trail I rode back over the ridge and signaled."

She was looking at Jerry. Linn whirled his horse and galloped down to the trail where it dipped down into the narrow gully that had to be crossed at an angle, it was so deep. There the road was dug out of the bank on either side, making a sharp elbow, and at the creek bank the gully widened to a small grassy coulee. The cattle coming down from the Shadow Mountain end of the Basin used this wash and the gully into which it ran. He wanted to see . . .

Sure enough, the sheep had crossed the road in the gully. But after them had gone cattle, trampling the tracks of the sheep. A man riding more or less at leisure, his eyes alert to any unusual sign along the way, would have noticed sheep droppings and the harrowed look of the ground. But who had ridden at leisure along that road lately?

Hoofbeats came pounding behind him, and he looked back and saw Billy coming down the wash. Linn

164

waited.

"Feller hadn't oughta go riding off alone, the way things are now, Linn," Billy reproved as he pulled up alongside. "What yuh lookin' for?"

"Looking to see just what kind of a deal this is. Does it strike you as a very strange coincidence, Billy, that a bunch of cattle should bring up the drag after a band of sheep?"

"Not unless they was drove. You can bank on that. So that ain't a coincidence."

"A man-made one, Bill. Two men, we'll say, to bring the cattle up the draw. At least two extra men flanking the sheep to keep them down here out of sight. Good Lord, this draw is a regular chute made to order! Somebody knows the lay of the land, in here, and don't you forget it."

"They must of been wise to a lot, Linn. Not knockin' the dead any—but you'd-a thought Paddy and Jim would of caught onto something. They sure didn't do any more ridin' than they had to. It was their job to keep cases on the Basin—and they let Eccleson get a camp half built and two bands of sheep located, before they woke up."

Linn's eyes reproached him for that, though all he said was. "Cabin fever's a bad thing, Bill. It had them both and it proved fatal. However this invasion got such a foothold, our job is to clean the Basin and keep it clean. Coleson's scrip papers ought to be forwarded before long—so he can shake them under Eccleson's nose as he demands."

Young McElroy twisted himself in the saddle and looked back. "Well, you're the boss, Linn, but—darn it, the sheep ain't down this draw, they're up it!"

For the first time that day Linn's humorous chuckle

was heard. "Spoiling for a fight, are you? Well, listen to me, old boy. There's more than sheep up this draw, and they've been there since yesterday morning. Half an hour more won't lose the fight—but it might possibly help to win it."

Billy looked glum. "I don't sabe this hanging back."

"You sabe finding out what we're up against, don't you? It looks as if Eccleson is deeper than John Coleson thinks: deeper and trickier. Those two thousand sheep he talked about needing range for are just the bait he used to keep us boys on the run while he got the rest nicely located in the Basin. I'm beginning to think he's shoving in every sheep he owns. That accounts for the size of the camp he's started, too."

"Well, what difference does that make?"

"Just this difference, Bill. They don't know it, but we're down to six men, and there's no telling how many Eccleson really has over here. I've counted six on this job right here, getting these sheep up this gully in a hurry and hazing a bunch of Triangle J cattle after them to cover the tracks. They turned our stock loose, above the road, and that's why Demmy saw sheep sign up there where she crossed the wash, and we didn't down here."

"Well, I'm equal to the hull six, the way I feel right now." Billy's grin was not mirthful.

"Not if they see you first. Count six that went in here, and the three that brought back our horses are nine, and whoever went up with the wagon Demmy thinks is back at their camp—those three we tangled with, probably. That makes just twelve men we'll have to assume are up ahead somewhere waiting for us."

He turned the bay and began to retrace their steps. "If you were in their place, Billy, where would you look for

166

us to show up?"

"Across that big meadow, I s'pose," Billy answered glumly.

"Exactly. From down this way, at least. And they certainly went to a heap of trouble to keep us from finding out about this band of sheep. We're supposed to think they're all out there on the flat, where Jerry and Miss Coleson saw them."

"So what you goin' to do now, Linn?"

"Get the boys and ride a wide circle north, and swing back along the foot of the mountain. Get in the back way. Locate this band of sheep and run them out—and I hope to thunder this chinook has rotted the ice so they'll do some swimming when they hit the creek!"

"We're liable to have our work cut out for us, if them twelve men don't take to the notion," Billy made dry comment.

But Linn was up the bank at a place where the slope was passable, scanning the ground for tracks. Presently he sent his horse down and across to the other side, rode along the gully's south bank, and returned in silence. They crossed the road, galloped on up the wash to where they had left Demmy, and found only a jumble of tracks, plainly leading up the Basin.

Linn was furious. He wondered what old Jerry was thinking about to let the girl ride straight up there into a trap and take the boys with her. Didn't they use their heads at all? Couldn't they understand that where these strange sheep went there would be extra men? They acted, he told himself carpingly, as if wrangling with that big Swede was all there was to it.

They were following the sheep tracks, and they must have been loitering along waiting for the two. Demmy was in the lead with Jerry and she turned her head away to scan the brushy head of the draw when Linn came pounding up, and seemed not to know or care that he had arrived.

Linn paid no attention to her. "Swing off this way, boys, and don't make all the noise you can. How about it, Jerry, can we ride straight north and keep under cover for a couple of miles?"

"Yeah, we can—what's up, Linn?"

"Plenty. And there'd have been more if you'd kept on the way you're headed." He glanced aside at the mountain, its bleak forbidding slopes looking dark and glowering under the humped peak standing bold against the racing clouds. As his gaze dropped to their immediate surroundings he met Demmy's bright cool eyes.

"The tracks go straight on up the Basin," she said in that aloof tone she had sometimes. "Aren't we going after the sheep, Mr. Moore?"

"We are, Miss Coleson. But if I may venture to suggest it, I think you should turn around and ride home. This isn't going to be any pink tea."

"No? I began to think it was, and we were considered a little too early to be polite."

"I think you'd find the reception committee ready and waiting to serve hot lead all around the minute we appear." And without waiting for whatever retort she might make to that he spurred ahead, motioning Billy and Red up alongside.

A girl like that, he thought wrathfully, could raise more hell than forty sheepmen on the fight. What he wanted to do was turn and ride out of that Basin and never come back, and if it were not for John Coleson, sick and worried and counting on him to settle this trouble as peaceably as possible, he would go right now;

168

or so he told himself.

What he did do was ride the long ellipse that held somewhere within it Eccleson's sheep and fighting crew—how many of either he could only guess— enough to make trouble for the Triangle J unless they were ousted before they had got too firm a foothold. By the number of cattle drifting down from the upper end of the Basin he had proof enough that they had been driven off their accustomed feeding grounds to make room for the sheep.

Because of the cattle he set a quiet pace, riding from thicket to thicket and avoiding the open meadows between, lest they be discovered and his plan be suspected before he could carry it out.

For a long nerve-racking hour he jogged along at a leisurely trot, certain that Demmy at least was fuming at the inaction. The wind had died to a summer-like breeze; just when it had ceased to blow a gale he could not recall, but he noticed it now because he had counted on the wind to cover the sound of their approach and to bring to their nostrils the telltale odor of dirty wool that would betray the whereabouts of the sheep.

Then, as he was thinking he had swung farther north than was necessary, the sound of axes out ahead made the horses lift heads to listen. Signing the others to wait, Linn rode forward at a cautious walk until the mutter of men's voices came to him. He left his horse, then, and went slipping through the sodden leaves of autumn that stilled his footsteps in the aspen grove whose lower end he knew. A little farther, and he saw . . .

The grove here grew close against a high sandstone cliff where the trees and brush were sparse in the barren soil. Huge boulders, scattered where they had fallen and rolled away from the bluffside in some primeval shake-

169

up, offered further protection, and the scanty brush had been cut and carried away from a considerable area, leaving open ground across which a jackrabbit could not hop unseen.

Linn stared in astonishment, heard a suppressed exclamation behind him, and whirled to find Demmy almost at his shoulder, Billy and Jerry not many yards away. And while he scowled at them he was nevertheless glad enough to have them there where they could see for themselves what he saw :

A wagon, piled high with camp supplies; and, snug within a breastwork of piled boulders, two tents set cannily close to where a spring ran out from a cleft in the rocks; men with rifles convenient to their hands at work clearing the site of new sheds, digging holes for corral posts—a small army, it looked to the startled gaze of those watchers from the Triangle J. An army alert, a sentinel posted down at the lower end of the clearing with a rifle leaning against the square brown boulder behind which he stood, his back exposed to the guns of the cowboys, had he but known it.

Linn beckoned the three and stole back out of hearing, walking with Indian quiet on the soft ground. And they had need of quiet. The air was so still down there under the cliff that sounds seemed magnified. The clink of a spade in a posthole when the metal struck rock; the sound of a man clearing his throat; a sneeze; muttered directions given by Eccleson himself, standing there in the middle of things bossing the job.

"Well," said Demmy in her quick impatient voice that betrayed how tense she was, "there they are. Up and at 'em, as somebody said in my history book." They were back with the horses and the three other men, and she looked from one to the other with eyes much too bright.

"There's a lovely setting for a most spectacular fight, boys."

"Talk sense, why don't you?" Linn stepped before her, almost brushing her aside as he went to his horse. "We're not going into the grave-digging business today, Miss Coleson." He met Red and Sandy's questioning looks with a tilt of his head toward the new camp. "Eccleson's there with twelve men by actual count. The way they've entrenched themselves they could hold off thirty and not half try."

"We goin' to leave them in possession, ye mean?" Sandy asked sourly.

"In possession of the boulders, yes. I'm willing to fight if it's necessary, but I hope I'm not a fighting fool. Our job is to protect—"

"Protect your own skin!" Demmy cut in, her voice two notes higher than Linn had ever heard it, with the metallic tone that threatened hysteria. "Why should you worry? Most of these men have their backs turned!"

Linn's breath almost hissed in through his teeth when they clamped shut. His nostrils flared, the skin around them white. His eyes were blued steel. Then he saw what was behind her fever-bright eyes and his own softened a little.

But not his voice. "You keep your mouth shut!" he said, all the more brutal because he spoke quietly. "You've no business here in the first place. In the second place, I happen to be working under your father's orders. You act like a spoiled kid that needs a good spanking, and if I hear any more out of you, that's what you'll get."

She lifted her hand to slap him across the mouth. Then it dropped and she burst into shrill hysterical laughter, rocking forward over the saddle horn.

171

Just for an instant, however. Then Linn had jumped his horse close alongside, and he had her by the shoulders, shaking her roughly. "Cut that out," he gritted, "or I'll slap you up to a peak! You want to bring Eccleson's outfit down on top of us right here?"

Demmy gasped, winced away from his threatening hand, hushed as suddenly as she had begun. Sanity looked out at him before her eyes brimmed with tears.

"You—you awful—brute!" she charged, but without conviction. Two deep uneven breaths and she had herself in hand, Linn watching her with a tense interest that would have passed for rage.

"Take her home, Jerry," he said shortly as he reined aside. "We can't have hysterics on our hands—along with everything else."

"I won't go," cried Demmy with a surprising calm. "I don't know what—happened to me. Jerry's going to stay on the job."

Linn gave her another long look, shrugged and turned away. "I'm going to locate those sheep and haze them back out of the Basin the way they came in. You fellows can stay and fight Eccleson if you feel that way. Suit yourselves."

He rode off, cutting across the ellipse. Whether they chose to follow or to stay behind with Demmy, he did not know. In the mood he was in he did not much care.

DRASTIC MEASURES

STRAIGHT FOR THE NEAREST little ridge Linn rode, mindful always of those armed sentinels behind the boulders a couple of hundred yards farther south. The next move must be wary, and it must be effective. The

172

third time had to be the last. He would make it the last, somehow. Barring the taking of human life, he was in the mood to stop at nothing: to kill the sheep that would eat the grass down to the very roots, their sharp little cloven hoofs cutting the sod like knives . . .

Kill the sheep? Kill the dogs too, if he had to. The situation had grown truly desperate for the Triangle J, already carrying trouble enough, what with the sickness of John Coleson and those three tragic deaths. There could be no bandying hard words now with Eccleson. This was a war that could hold no compromise. Either the sheep or the cattle must go; there was no room in Shadow Mountain Basin for both.

In the soft, snow-moistened ground on the slope his bay's shod hoofs scored deep tracks. He did not look back to see how many of the boys had followed, yet when he reached the crest and stopped to reconnoiter, the others pulled up so close behind him that he was only the length of his horse removed from the group. From the tail of his eye he saw that even Demmy was there, looking white and spent, old Jerry watching her solicitously. The girl was all in, wrought up to the breaking point. He ought to have known . . .

"They're hugging close to shelter," Billy observed, moving up beside Linn, his thoughts apparently concerned only with the sheep.

"It's some help to know where they're not," Linn answered with a mirthless half-smile. "I think we'd better scatter out and search all the coulees—or swales, they are really. They've got to be down east of here, I think. We know too well those draws against the south wall. They wouldn't get out too far north, because they have to keep in touch with that camp."

He turned abruptly to the others. "Any of you boys

173

smell sheep?"

Gravely they sniffed the air like hunting dogs, and as gravely confessed that they did not. Linn stifled a brief grin and pointed a gloved finger.

"They're over there, then. They can't be anywhere else. When we swung north we were too far this side, and the wind carried the sound and smell of them the other way. As Billy just said, they're keeping under cover."

His sharp glance swept their faces, consciously avoided meeting Demmy's shadowed eyes, and came back to the rough yet wonderfully fertile terrain spread out before them.

"We'll ride together to the first little coulee and see if that's the place. We may need to separate after that, unless we find them."

Without more words they reached the coulee's edge, found it empty. Linn took three men and left Jack and Sandy with old Jerry and Demmy, and scouted farther north, looking and listening for the sharp yelp of dogs. They must be in there somewhere, he kept telling himself worriedly. Those fresh tracks couldn't lie. But if they were back on the south side, within sound of the camp—well, getting them out from under the rifles of those twelve men was not going to be so simple.

They were leaving the next ridge, meaning to ride down a wide draw opening out below them, when a long halloo came faintly from behind. Linn pulled up short, twisting himself in the saddle to look. On the rim of the first coulee a man stood out in sharp relief against the slate-blue clouds, waving them back. His hat swung in long arcs over his head. The sheep, that hat said, had been found.

"Down here about a mile," Jack yelled as they came

loping up. "I didn't see 'em myself, but Demmy did. I turned back when the stink got so strong it near knocked me off'n my horse." And he added matter-of-factly, "Jerry sure was on the warpath when I left. Wouldn't 'sprise me none if he's tangled with the herders by now."

As if his words were a signal, down the shallow coulee and around a turn a gun popped, then another. With a sudden tightness in his chest as if something had gripped him there, Linn wheeled and sent his horse recklessly down the precipitous side hill. After him tore the others. Three guns were barking like angry dogs . . .

They thundered down the coulee bottom, their horses flinging up chunks of yellow soil as they went. So abruptly it caught them almost unawares, they whipped around the turn and were upon the scene.

Across the coulee, filling it from bank to bank, huddled the sheep, a gray woolly carpet rippling with movement and yet stationary there. Running back and forth, holding the sheep yet bewildered and without orders, were the dogs. And from behind rocks on the farther side of the band rifles began to pop—more rifles than two herders could handle.

At the point of the elbow sat Demmy on her horse, barely out of sight and able to chance a shot now and then from a vantage point between two rock outcroppings. Sandy and Jerry were down behind the lowest shoulder of rock, methodically shooting into the massed sheep.

Theoretically Linn had determined to do it, himself; actually the sight made him wince. And yet, it was sheep and dogs, or the men . . . And the sheep were giving way, while their herders crouched there sending futile shots toward the point.

Old Jerry cocked an eye up at Linn. "We got 'em cold, boy," he exulted. "I hate to do it, but I'm gonna start in on the dogs. The sheep's about ready to stampede back down the coulee right now—"

"All right," Linn agreed shortly, his mouth bitter. "Put 'em on the run, boys. The men will have to go with the sheep—and they certainly—"

"I can't shoot dogs!" cried Demmy tragically. "I'd rather shoot a herder!"

"Pity you wouldn't rather go home where you belong," Linn snapped as he rode past. "All right, boys, call this the dead line. Never mind the men—I'll watch them. But put the sheep back down this coulee and into that draw they came up, or drop them in their tracks!"

It was not pretty work, though in his heart Linn knew it was a kindness to the sheep—certainly to the dogs, which knew little of comfort or kindness while they lived. At the very start Demmy weakened and rode back where she could not see what was happening, and sat on a rock with her head buried in her arms.

Linn did not know that. He was off across the coulee, slipping up on the herders from behind, edging forward to the brow of the thirty-foot bank where he could look down upon them where they huddled behind their chosen boulders, shooting across at the point. Four men, crouching almost within arm's length of one another, the sheep spread across the coulee before them.

Fools. Idiots, to bunch up like that. They showed as little sense as the sheep. Eccleson had hired poor stuff to drive his wedge into the Basin, Linn thought, as he stood up and got the center man lined up with the front sight of his rifle.

"Drop—those—guns!"

Rifles clattered against the rocks as the four jumped

176

and goggled up at him. Linn could have laughed at the stark incredulity in their faces; but he did not, even when their hands went reaching above their heads.

"Stand up and march out of there. Follow your sheep back where they came from. Or, wait a minute!" And he yelled across for Billy, who jumped on his horse and came on the run.

"Search these lamb-lickers for six-guns," he called down tersely. "Then get them moving. You fellows follow on down to the draw and see to it the sheep cross the creek—if they have to swim!"

"You betcha!" And Billy hopped off and searched the four to their boots, gleaning four knives and one six-shooter from the lot.

"All right, Bill, turn them loose. They can head for Eccleson's camp if they like, and tell him next time it won't be the dogs or the sheep we'll go after."

"And then what?" Billy tilted his head back, wrinkled his nose and stared up grinning. "When do we eat? Or don't we?"

"Just as soon as the sheep are across the creek. I'm going to do a little scouting. See you at camp . . ."

He waved his hand and was gone, riding away to examine all draws to the southward.

LINN PLAYS A HUNCH

REACTION HAD SEIZED LINN, sent him riding at last to the line camp at a loafing walk, his hands folded on the saddle horn and his whole body slumped in the slackness of a weariness that strikes into the very soul. The sheep, minus dogs and herders, were scattering out to aimless grazing beyond the Cherry Creek, running

177

here and there amongst the little draws and gulches that ran like spread fingers down the flats to the bank. Days would be spent in gathering them again, and no doubt there would be greater loss than the few the boys had shot, but that could not be helped. Eccleson had had his warning and he had known what to expect. The sheep were his affair.

Linn did not worry about the sheep. He did not worry about anything in particular. He was dead-tired, and nothing mattered a hoot, so far as he was concerned. He was so apathetic he even went without a smoke for some time before he took the trouble to make one. When he did finally, and lighted it, he held the match absently between thumb and finger and watched it burn with scarcely a flicker. If you made a wish, and the match burned entirely without breaking, your wish would come true . . .

Ah, hell! What was the use of wishing, even if there was anything worth wishing for? He flipped the burnt stub into a bush, saw it go black as it fell. Something queer about that too, if it mattered enough to think what it was. It didn't. Nothing did. You lived along from day to day and let yourself get all stirred up over things, and then you reached the end and discovered that nothing mattered at all. Not a—damned—thing. Or if it did, it never came out right, so what was the use?

Nothing was the use when he threw a leg over the cantle and stepped down from his horse at the cabin door. Well, maybe he was hungry—a little; since he hadn't eaten since before daylight he should be pretty ravenous, but even hunger failed to interest him much. The stovepipe was sending up heat wrinkles in the air—straight up, like the match . . .

Attention arrested, pricked a little with awareness of

178

something he should be considering, he halted and gazed around him at the still bushes that had whipped so lately in the gale that wiped out the snow. Not a breath of wind, now. Well, maybe that was what ailed him. There was a mugginess in the air; low pressure. It sure as hell pressed him down with it.

In the doorway Red stood grinning at him. "Well, boss, we sure put the kibosh on the sheep! 'Dja see 'em spread out across the creek?" And when he saw Linn look inquiringly past him he added, "Billy and the rest went up to finish fillin' the graves." His young eyes sobered as he looked up toward the cottonwoods, where three horses stood drooping, apparently gazing at their bridle reins dropped to the ground. "I'd 'a went, but there wasn't much to do."

Because Linn stood there without speaking, Red got out the makings and, settling his shoulders against the casing, proceeded with the business of rolling a cigarette. "Sure turned off still," he remarked. "Wouldn't s'prise me if we git a storm. If we do, them sheep—"

"Did everybody come on here to camp?" A ripple had shot through Linn's nerves. "Where's Jerry?"

Red licked down his cigarette. "Him? He's poundin' his ear on Paddy's bunk. Supper'll be ready pretty quick. I shoveled hay into the mangers, Linn. Thought mebbe you'd want the horses all kep' up tonight, so I didn't turn any of 'em out." He drew a match along the wall beside him.

"That's all right. Tell Jerry I'm going on back to the ranch, will you? I'll be down in the morning. John will want to know what all—"

"Demmy, she just left a while ago," Red very casually remarked. "She stayed on till the last dog was

179

hung—till we got the sheep across; and then she struck out for home . . ." Words hung unspoken in his voice; words even Red could not speak when Linn's face had just that look.

"All right; tell the boys to look for me in the morning." Linn started for the corral, leading his horse.

"Ain't you goin' to wait for supper?"

"I'll eat at the ranch," Linn vouchsafed over his shoulder, and did not see Red's grin of understanding. He was concerned only with his need to hurry, and wondering impatiently why that need should seem so pressing; why he wanted a fresh horse; why minutes counted . . .

The weather—yes, the weather had a strange ominous hush, as if it were waiting for a storm to break. But he could not wait, and therein lay the strangeness. Demmy? Well, the girl had no business to ride off alone like that, feeling the way she did. You couldn't tell Linn that she wasn't on the edge of a collapse. Hysterical, back there—and she probably wasn't feeling any better now. She was trying to hide her feelings, but Pollo getting shot like that had hit her hard; a damn sight harder than she would ever let on . . . And her snubbing him the way she had been doing since she came home didn't make her feel any better now.

Well, he supposed he was uneasy over the girl, going off like that on a fifteen-mile ride alone. Safe enough—if it stormed, it probably wouldn't come before night; sometime before morning, probably, unless the wind blew up again from the southwest . . . No, it was Demmy herself. She might faint and fall off her horse, or something.

By the time he had reached that definite conclusion Linn had his saddle on a fresh horse and was on his way. The air was so still a feather would have fallen straight to earth. Still and warm, with a balminess of spring. He felt the hazy warmth on his face as he galloped steadily down the Basin trail—creating a breeze with the speed he traveled, boring steadily into that muggy quiet.

Out of the Basin and up the long hill to the level bench, his eyes searching the trail ahead for a rider, he let his heels tilt the rowels against the sweaty flanks of his horse. The bench was not the flat plane it looked from a distance, of course. When you rode over it you crossed scallops large and small, and there were wind-gouged hollows where the soil was pocketed with sand and grass roots would not sod. A horseman might be half the time concealed in some such depression . . .

His eyes moved away, drawn to the bold outline of Shadow Mountain. It looked painted against a queer dingy gray wall that seemed to press in upon it. Snow. All the north sky banked with it, bulging like a blown curtain, waiting only for the wind . . .

Linn looked no more that way, but pulled his coat together and buttoned it to his chin, yanked his hat down tight over his straight dark brows and jabbed the spurs deep. In the night sometime? Lord, it was a matter of minutes now! And when it struck the bench . . .

So this was what had pushed him, urged him, compelled him to hurry on home without waiting for his supper. This was the worry and the fear: not the remote possibility that Demmy Coleson might faint and fall off her horse, but the fear that she might be caught in the deadly grip of a blizzard such as the northern ranges know too well.

And she would be. As he leaned to his horse's flying mane and tore along the trail, flashing in and out of

181

those earth waves like an antelope bounding away from the hunter's gun, he glimpsed her riding over a small crest, perhaps a mile ahead. Riding slowly—taking no thought of the dire presage hovering there behind the mountain; not the Black One she pretended to fear, but a raging white demon poised ready to pounce.

But in another minute she must see what threatened. The road swung west, then north around the end of a wrinkle that ages ago had been gouged down deep where the hardpan had faulted. "Black Gulch," the boys called it. She must swing there, keeping the smoother stretch between the gulch and Dry Wash still farther north.

Eight miles they called it from Black Gulch to the ranch house; seven to the line camp. Maybe she could make it if she woke up that horse of hers and got a little speed out of him. Dreaming along the trail with a blizzard coming—you would think a girl raised in this country would have more sense. Hot anger surged up at her heedlessness; anger that forgot how he had loafed along, not so far back.

She made the turn alongside the gulch, riding toward the mountain, parallel to him now, with rough spiny outcroppings of rock scattered through the half-mile stretch between. Too far to call and be heard, too rough to ride across; so he pulled his gun and fired three shots into the air as he raced along.

Her horse heard, but Demmy herself paid no attention. Too far, and now puffs of cold air blew down across the mountain and over the prairie. No, she wouldn't hear unless she was listening for some such sound. Linn spurred his grunting horse to a longer stride and whipped around the bend at the gulch as if he were turning a cow that had bolted from the herd.

But now that cold wind struck him like ice water, stinging his face. (She'd feel that, darn her!) One blast, another, and the white smother of snow swept down upon them, blotting out the world.

Linn bowed to it, turning his face away; closing his eyes to slits, trying to see through his clogged lashes. The horse slowed, tried to swerve away, and was kicked into his stride again, an iron hand holding him to the trail. Lips stretched in a grin that had no more meaning than a mask, Linn shielded his eyes as well as he could with his hat brim and squinted ahead into the white smother. His spurs raked deep through wet hair, urging the horse forward . . .

It seemed an hour, but it could not have been more than a minute of that blind seeking. Then a vague shape wavered before him and was gone; showed again, close. His horse slackened and swerved, shortening its stride to a lope, a slow trot like a machine running down. The shape became Demmy, bowed over the saddle horn, trying to shield her face with one arm as she rode.

STORM WITHOUT, JOY WITHIN

SHE DID NOT HEAR HIM come up alongside; with her face turned away she did not see him nor know he was there until he called her name. Both horses were sidling, trying to turn tails to the terrific blast of snow and icy wind. Linn thought swiftly, made up his mind.

"We can't make it! Here, give me your reins!" he shouted, and swung off.

"What—are you going to do?" Demmy's voice

sounded muffled, as if under a blanket. He fumbled, got her horse by the bridle, pulled one rein down, and swung both horses around in the trail, facing back the way they had come. It was the only thing he could do. No living thing could face that storm and survive for very long.

Fine as bolted flour, the snow was an impalpable white wall driven forward on the gale sweeping out of the north. No world save the storm and themselves existed. Already the horses were white effigies—manes, tails, and saddle-creases packed with snow. Demmy was a blurred white shape in the saddle, shoulders drawn up to protect her neck where the wind searched cruelly to drive that chill packing.

With the blizzard at their back the breathing was better, the swirling snow less suffocating. The horses stepped out briskly, tugging at the reins, wanting to run from the blizzard they could not meet. Against wind and their eager push Linn braced his legs and tried to keep the road he could no longer see. Tried to remember small landmarks; tried to judge distance, direction, time and endurance.

"You're not trying to get back to camp, I hope," cried Demmy above the whoop of the wind. "We'll never make it, Linn."

Strange, Linn thought even then, how antagonisms are lost in danger. He did not answer, at least not in words. By a sudden drop in the trail he made a desperate guess at their exact position and swung sharply to the left, the blizzard greeting that change with a fierce fling and hiss of snow against their cheeks.

Demmy was answered. A little farther and she was down standing beside him against a rock ledge, the blizzard sweeping low over their heads, feeling for them, tossing swirls of snow in their faces as it went ravening on over the prairie.

"Hold the horses. I can build up a windbreak with these loose rocks. Soon as the snow packs in the chinks it'll be shelter."

"Anchor your horse with a rock, then. I'm not going to stand here and freeze my feet—"

And a while later, as they stood huddled together in the poor shelter they had made for themselves, she said tentatively, "I know this place. I killed a rattlesnake here, one summer. There's brush— sagebrush— straight out ahead there."

He leaned and peered, shook his head dubiously. "I'd better try and scramble some along this ledge where I won't get lost. Ten yards out there is good as a mile . . ."

Suddenly he gave a short laugh. "Wait. Have you got a rope?"

"Why—yes, of course. What—"

"Dakota clothesline. My dad used to tell about it." He went to the saddles, came back knotting two ropes together. "You hold one end and haul me back— figuratively speaking."

Strangely, his weariness had gone completely. He did not feel now that nothing mattered. Some things did. They mattered a great deal. Getting a fire for Demmy mattered more than anything in all his life . . .

Until dark and long after, Linn fought the blizzard and wallowed and scrambled, pawing through, the deepening drifts for the stunted sage that grew among the rocks; fought his way back when his shout set Demmy pulling in the rope hand-over-hand.

A great girl, Demmy. She wasn't taking any chance of letting the rope slide through her hands and go snaking out into the storm when he pulled too hard,

185

reaching for more brush. Not much she wasn't. She had tied it to her saddle horn, and she had the horse tied to a rock. Not that he would have left that ledge, poor brute. They were both too glad to have the shelter and the company.

Later there was fire under the ledge; a feeble, flickering blaze kept alive with niggardly handfuls of pungent gnarled branches. Not much of a fire, ever. A fire whose tiny sparks were gobbled down by the shrieking demon of wind and snow; a fire that showed them how wild was the night around them, out there where the smoke went whipping away into the white swirl . . .

But when they sat close together on one saddle blanket, the other wrapped warm over their laps, with their backs to the ledge and their feet to the little blaze, and with their blood racing young and glowing in their veins—why then it was quite snug in their shelter. Some mysterious alchemy of the fire welded thoughts together, burning out resentments and the like. It may have been midnight when they finally reached the mystery that had thrown them into such discord, but reach it they did, in an abrupt fashion like this:—

"I want to say something, Linn. You're so—so quick to misjudge—"

"*I'm* quick to misjudge?"

"Well—you shouldn't hold me to what I said there at the cabin. The—the shock of walking in there and finding . . ." She paused, staring into the fire. "And of course, I knew you two hated each other . . ." Another pause which Linn made no attempt to break.

So she turned and looked at him in the orange glow of the fire. "I wasn't looking for evidence against you, you know," she said, in an odd tone of constraint. "I was—

186

eliminating any possible suspicion that might attach to you later on, if—if the murderer isn't found."

"You—*what?*"

"I was proving you *didn't* do it. After Sandy brought up the possibility—well, I'm Dad's eyes and ears, out away from the house. There has to be someone who represents the owner, in ways not concerned with the work. Someone to assume the responsibility—"

"That, of course. So how did you prove I didn't do it?" Linn hated this. For a while he had forgotten all about Pollo and his incredible death. For a while he had just been Linn Moore taking care of Demmy Coleson caught out in the worst blizzard he had seen for ages, keeping her safe and as comfortable as harsh circumstances would permit. He wished she didn't feel she had to talk about that thing. But since he must— "You couldn't prove anything."

"I could prove there wasn't any of that kind of gun oil at the line camp, couldn't I? Sandy's a great old Scotty, but once an idea gets into his head you've simply got to blast it out with proof he's wrong." She shivered, and Linn poked burning twigs together and laid a stick across them.

"Well, did you blast out that one?"

"I shall, when I have a chance to talk to him. Red and Jack say there wasn't anything of the sort, too. And even Sandy couldn't find a thing to bolster up the theory." She looked at him sidelong. "You didn't have to take it for granted I was trying to make a case against you, Linn. That gun business last night—I only wanted to get the facts all down on record while they were fresh in everyone's mind. Of course I knew—"

"Knew what?" At that moment, when Linn wanted to look into her eyes, she stared persistently out into the

187

shifting white wall beyond the little fire. "What did you know, Demmy?"

"I knew you never in this world could have shot Pollo. It—well, it just isn't in you to do a thing like that. In a fight, maybe—" She found a stick, leaned and poked the fire unnecessarily. "So," she added briskly, "I merely wanted to prove it."

"But, Demmy girl—"

"Don't let's talk about it!" she cried in a hushed yet broken voice. "Let's just keep—everybody out of here!"

She could not have known just what effect that would have, nor could Linn until sanity came back to him and he wondered when and how Demmy came into his arms, his face against her cheek.

That was some minutes later, when the fire threatened to die down and Linn was obliged to free one arm and lay wood on the coals. Demmy laughed a little, and remarked that this was great weather for a proposal, and wasn't Linn afraid of a cool reception?

Linn declared that he was not, and that the weather suited him exactly. They talked foolishly, and laughed a good deal, softly and with their heads close together—and scarcely noticed how the snow was piling into the hollow just before the ledge. For the matter of that, they could not see much of it, because the two horses, standing close by, blocked all view of the opening to the east; and the piled windbreak to the west grew higher and thicker as the hours passed.

They even sang together before the gray daylight came to show them how great was their plight. They sang, and Demmy practised yodeling and always ended with laughter. But they did not sing *"O Sole Mio"* in any language whatever, and Linn did not yodel that there was an echo in the valley. Without another word

188

on the subject they kept that time for themselves, death and all trouble walled out by the storm.

BARRIERS DOWN

"BUT WE'VE GOT TO talk about it, Demmy girl." Linn had tramped the snow down in their little retreat, letting the drift pile high out front. Actually they were now in a crude wind-made igloo, a comb of hard-packed snow jutting out from the ledge above their heads, the rock windbreak buried deep. By his watch it was ten minutes past noon, and the storm showed no sign of slackening.

But they were warm in their snow hut with the horses standing heads to the fire and adding the heat of their strong bodies to the meager warmth of the fire which Linn managed to keep alive. He used twigs now, bits of bark, nursing it jealously, as much for its cheerfulness as anything. It was a link between this white chaos and their warm, full-fed world. It at least gave them something to watch, made their refuge less bleak.

"We've got to talk this thing out between us," he insisted again later that afternoon, after he had floundered out into the drifts and blowing snow and had gleaned the last bit of brush he could find. "I've got to tell you something, my dear."

She gave him a startled look. "What is it, Linn?"

"Just that I couldn't marry you while this is hanging over me. People will whisper and guess and—you know how it would be. It will always be in men's minds that I must have killed Pollo and was cute enough to get away with it."

"It isn't in my mind, nor in Dad's—nor Billy's nor Red's nor Jerry's. I don't know about the others, but I can show them how you couldn't have done it. That ought to be enough—"

"It isn't enough for me, Demmy girl. It happened, we know that. And until I've found out how it happened—" He knelt and took her in his arms again. "Oh, Girl, the marriage is—well, it's off, that's all. I can't tie you up to a man they say—"

"They say nothing!" Demmy's hand went up, brushing snow off his hat brim with a movement that was a caress. "And I'm compromised within an inch of my reputation this minute, Mr. Moore. Aren't you going to give me the protection of your name, after—"

"Be quiet!" His brows came together. "You know darned good and well—"

"Yes, dear." Her tone was altogether too meek to be sincere. "I know lots of things good and well. Darned good and well." She sobered abruptly. "I know how you feel about—that. But that has nothing to do with our getting married."

"I can't—not until I know how that happened."

"All right." She settled back against his shoulder and tucked her feet under the blanket. "We're bright. We've had booklarning, and we may possibly have learned to think things out." She tucked in a lock of hair that had worked out from .under her cap. "I could think better if I weren't so hungry," she sighed.

"We'll eat a horse if we're held up here another week," Linn promised. "Forget it."

"I could eat them both right now, if we had salt," Demmy sighed lugubriously. "Won't you really and truly marry me unless—?"

"Such grammar! No, honest, I've been about half crazy, trying to think—"

"I thought about Jim. Contraction—"

"I thought of that. The way he was holding his gun, pointed toward the door. And Pollo was close to the bunk. It wouldn't happen once in a thousand times, I suppose, but still—"

"It *could* happen, Linn! I've thought and thought, and that's about the only way—"

Linn shook his head with gloomy finality. "Paddy put the kibosh on that idea, though. Jim's gun was empty—they shot it out with each other. Don't you remember?"

"I—I was thinking more about you," she confessed. "Yes, I remember—I think I do." She sighed. "There's another thing, of course. Jim's gun was a double-action, and they pull harder, you know. I remember the boys were talking about it one Sunday last spring, when we were all doing target practice out in the meadow. So—well, maybe a doctor could tell us . . ."

"Jim's gun was light on the trigger. We can test that out. He and Paddy were quarreling about that, the day we mixed those two bands of sheep. Jim had filed it—they had quite an argument. Paddy claimed it was dangerous. Maybe it was; maybe that's what their last quarrel was about."

Demmy sat up straight. "Then it was Jim's gun that shot Pollo. Linn dear, I'm absolutely positive! Think hard. When you went in, wasn't there any smoke coming out of Jim's gun?"

Linn shook his head regretfully. "Like a chump I waited to pop whoever came out. I lost a full minute or more, you remember. No, I didn't see any smoke coming out of his gun or any other. And anyway, he and Paddy emptied their guns at each other. You ought to remember that; you signed as a witness."

"Yes, of course. I remember how formal Mother made the statement sound; not at all like Paddy." She

191

wrinkled her brows, puzzling over something.

Suddenly she clutched his arm. "Linn! Don't you remember just what Paddy said? Can't you? Because it was Mother who wrote 'James Caplan fired six shots at me, wounding me fatally.' I remember that, it sounded so stilted and queer. But Linn, what was it Paddy actually said? *He* didn't say Jim fired six shots at him, wounding him fatally—I simply cannot conceive of Paddy saying that. Oh, what *did* he say? Think, Linn—think!"

Holding her close to him, Linn sent his thoughts questing back like hounds on an old trail. Paddy, making labored effort to gloss his own part in the duel. Paddy saying there was a look in Jim's eye—what was it, now?

"He said—when I asked him if he had killed Jim, the first shot—he said, 'Hell, no! I spoiled his aim for him' and then—by Jove, Demmy! He said, 'Jim was a good shot—so I stood and shot it out.' And he went on about meeting Jim in hell, and how they'd start in where they left off."

"And that was simply Mother's neat and dignified translation, saying: 'Jim fired six shots, wounding me fatally.' Oh, Linn, my dear, I believe we've got the answer. I believe there was a shot left in Jim's gun, and when the muscles and tendons began to stiffen, his fingers squeezed the trigger. Don't you see?" Her voice was jubilant. "That's exactly what happened. Since you didn't do it, and no one else had been near the cabin after Paddy left, that's the only way it *could* have happened. So there," she finished with a sigh of relief, "you have the answer to the mystery."

Linn disengaged his arm and replenished the tiny fire on its small bed of coals within its circle of bare ground. He did not look so happy as perhaps he should. When

192

he sat back again he spoke his thought.

"The solution, maybe. But we'll be a heck of a long while proving it. What shall I do? Go kill me a man and lay him out with a gun in his fist, and stand around and wait to see what happens?"

"No," said Demmy calmly enough, in spite of her involuntary shiver at the picture his words painted. "No, I think not. I think, if this storm ever clears up, you can go down and count the bullet holes in the front wall, in line with Jim's gun as he was holding it."

Linn sat still as the rock ledge behind him. Then a smile lighted his eyes, swept down to his handsome mouth, set his whole face aglow. "I'll give up," he chuckled. "I see I'm going to have to marry you. You've fenced the last way out!" And with that he gathered her close within his arms.

The wind shrieked and it howled and it flung the snow hissing through the air. It thinned the air tantalizingly, then stirred it thick as porridge again. It gouged out the drift before them, swinging to the west that it might claw their shelter down . . .

They knew nothing of all that. The ravings of the wind they never heard. Heads close together, cold cheek against cheek, they were very busy planning their wedding supper, arguing at great length over the oysters on the half shell—Linn wanting to get at the twenty pound turkey without waste of time. They wrangled over dessert—Demmy wanting plum pudding, Linn holding out for hot mince pie with a slab of cheese as big (so he declared) as a saddle blanket.

So the wind, failing to win any notice whatever or even to drive fear into their hearts where joy held full possession, gave a final prolonged *"Whew-w-w-w!"* and laid himself down on the snow, patting it gently to rest.

ALL CLEAR AHEAD

OLD JERRY LIFTED FROM his bench at the table as if he had been jabbed with a pin. "Well, for g-a-w-s-h sake!" he gasped, eyes bulging. "Where in time did you two come from? Ain't wallowed clear over from the ranch?"

Red and Billy, springing to clear a gangway to the stove, collided and blocked the path. Demmy staggered a little, leaning a hand on Jerry's shoulder.

But she laughed, albeit shakily. "No, only halfway from the ranch. You haven't anything to eat, I suppose?"

Voices exclaiming together created sympathetic uproar.

"I was kinda worried—but the boys was sure you had time to make it in ahead of the storm," Jerry finally wedged into the noise. "What yuh come back down here for? Wasn't you closer to home? Red and Jack, you go put up their horses. Where you been, anyway?" And when they had told him, both talking at once, he came back to the query, "What yuh come back here for? Facin' that cold wind—you'd 'a had it in your back from the Gulch on in to the ranch . . ."

"We came," Demmy said clearly, "to count bullet holes."

"Hunh?"

"No, Linn, wait. You boys hurry and take care of our poor horses, and come back here. We'll eat and then tell you . . . Don't deceive me, Bobwhite—do I smell roast beef?"

"Yeah—the boys, they butchered a long yearlin' that come in to the c'rell. Wait. Lemme pour yuh some coffee. I bet you're both half starved . . ."

"In a good cause, my good man. You wait. Linn, did you ever smell such coffee and such food in your life?"

Jerry watched them, cuddling his pipe in one bony palm. "Gittin' storm-stayed out at Black Gulch sure seems to agree with yuh, Demmy," he remarked dryly at last. "You looked like a string of suckers when you left here yesterday . . ."

Demmy blushed. "I needed to get good and hungry once," she evaded. "It was worth it. We—Linn and I are sure we solved the mystery, Jerry. Soon as we finish—if I ever do! — we'll try and prove it to all of you—"

Jerry looked from one to the other. "Don't have to prove it to me," he said gruffly. "What's the great strain to show proof, all of a sudden? Ain't Linn's word good enough?"

"No, it isn't," Linn spoke for the first time. "I want it proved beyond all possible doubt."

"Oh." Jerry busied himself over his pipe.

"I'll be fair glad to see ye prove it," Sandy declared seriously. "I like ye fine, lad, but the thing has me worried. I'll not deny it."

"That being the case—come in, boys—you tell them, will you, Linn? I can't wait any longer." Demmy got up and stood beside Linn, her cheeks very red—though that may have been from the cold ride—and her eyes very bright, which had nothing to do with the weather.

" . . . And so, unless there has been a lot of shooting done in here, one time and another—"

"None that I know of," Jerry cut in. "Only tenderfeet fiddle with guns in the house. Go ahead."

"From Jim's position, and what Paddy said, he did all his shooting from the bed. Pollo fell in front of the bunk, and the bullet went clear through him. You all know that."

Several heads nodded acquiescence.

195

"His gun was empty, and you can test for yourselves how light the trigger pull is. Pretty light, according to Paddy. So, if you can find where Jim's bullets hit the wall, and Paddy's—"

"I getcha!" Billy whirled and began searching the wall behind him. Heads bent, shoulders crowded together.

"Here," Sandy leaned forward to hold something out to Billy. "Stick a match in the hole and ye can line them up betterrr."

Half an hour later they looked at Linn, eyes warm and friendly. Sandy thrust out his hand. "I hated to think it, lad—but proof is proof," he growled, and wondered why Demmy should laugh like that.

"God bless that blizzard," Linn exclaimed under his breath, but with a fervency that made them all look at him. "Gave us time to think it out, boys. But most of all—" his eyes went to meet the girl's—"It—"

"Ah, we can say it for yuh, and we won't stutter over it the way you do," laughed Billy. "I could of told yuh that you two was figuring on a weddin', when you put your noses in the door!"

"Damn right," grunted Red.

"So I cooks us up a big supper," Bobwhite was inspired to say. "Git back outa the way, you fellers. I got t' have room . . ."

The sheep problem? There was no sheep problem after that blizzard was finished with the range. And before another such problem could arise in the Basin, the Triangle J had legal authority to put up fences, wave the Government papers which Eccleson demanded, and otherwise show their right of possession.

Bertha Muzzy Bower, born in Cleveland, Minnesota, in 1871, was the first woman to make a career of writing Western fiction and remains one of the most widely known, having written nearly seventy novels. She became familiar with cowboys and ranch life at sixteen when her family moved to the Big Sandy area of Montana. She was nearly thirty and mother of three before she began writing under the surname of the first of her three husbands. Her first novel, *Chip, of the Flying U*, was initially published as a serial in 1904 and was an immediate success. Bower went on to write more books, fourteen in all, about the Flying U, one of the best being the short story collection, *The Happy Family*. In 1933 she turned to stories set prior to the events described in *Chip, of the Flying U*. *The Whoop-up* actually begins this saga, recounting Chip Bennett's arrival in Montana and at the Flying U. Much of the appeal of this saga is due to Bower's use of humor, the strong sense of loyalty and family depicted among her characters, as well as the authentic quality of her cowboys. She herself was a maverick who experimented with the Western story, introducing modern technologies and raising unusual social concerns—such as aeroplanes in *Skyrider* or divorce in *Lonesome Land*. She was sensitive to the lives of women on the frontier and created some extraordinary female characters, notably in Vada Williams in *The Haunted Hills*, Georgie Howard in *Good Indian*, Helen in *The Bellehelen Mine*, and Mary Allison in *Trouble Rides the Wind*, another early Chip Bennett story. She was also able to write Western novels memorable for the characterization of setting and dramatization of nature, such as *Van Patten* or *The Swallowfork Bulls*.